≠
T661t

Their House

Books by Mary Towne

Wanda the Worrywart
Their House

THEIR HOUSE

Mary Towne

Atheneum   1990   New York

Atheneum
Macmillan Publishing Company
866 Third Avenue
New York, New York 10022
Collier Macmillan Canada, Inc.
First Edition
Printed in the United States of America
10 9 8 7 6 5 4 3 2 1
Designed by Nancy Williams

Library of Congress Cataloging-in-Publication Data
Towne, Mary.
Their house / Mary Towne. — 1st ed.
p. cm.
Summary: Moving into their new, more spacious house, Molly's
parents regret their decision to let the former owners, an elderly
couple, stay on until they find a place of their own.
ISBN 0-689-31562-7
[1. Moving, Household—Fiction. 2. Dwellings—Fiction. 3. Old
age—Fiction.] I. Title.
PZ7.T6495Th 1990 [Fic]—dc20 89-34969 CIP AC

For Lucy

Their House

ONE

"WELL, KIDS, HERE we are."

Dad drove slowly along the wet blacktop, past a tall evergreen hedge on the right, then nosed the car between rain-streaked granite posts onto a narrow gravel driveway that sloped away downhill. He switched the engine off but left the windshield wipers going. "Won't hurt to stop for just a minute," he told Mom when she looked at him questioningly. "So guys—what do you think?"

Because of the hedge, Molly hadn't been able to see much more of the house from the road than a long slate roof gleaming like a mussel shell in the cold March rain. But anyway, she told herself, it didn't matter what they thought, she and Sean. Her parents had already made up their minds. Maybe she wouldn't even bother to look.

But of course she did, pressing up against Sean on the backseat to gaze through the rain-fogged window. She'd been expecting a tall white colonial, the kind with black shutters and maybe even columns. But this house had a front of plain gray stone, small blocks fitted together so smoothly you could hardly see where they joined, and square diamond-paned windows that were set flat into the stone, without ledges. Halfway along, between three downstairs windows on either side, was a wide front door with a rounded top, painted a solid dark blue. There didn't seem to be any front yard, just brick paving in the space between the house and the hedge, with circles left out for trees and bushes. The bricks looked old, Molly thought, small and soft-colored and uneven, so that the rain bounced off them in little twinkling spurts.

"It looks . . . foreign," she said. Different was what she meant, and not necessarily in a bad way. But it was the wrong word to choose.

"Oh, come on, Molly," Dad said. "I know you're not crazy about the idea of moving, but this is still just Dayton, Connecticut, okay? In fact"—he glanced at the dashboard—"only a mile and seven-tenths from Hubbard Street. We could do a lot of the hauling ourselves when the time comes," he said to Mom. "Use the station wagon, and just hire a small van for the heavy stuff."

"I know what Molly means," Sean said unexpectedly. "All those dark bushes." He meant the tall ones around the side of the house, where light from a corner window glistened on a mass of glossy, pointed leaves. "And the cobblestones."

"Cobblestones?" Mom laughed. "Oh, Sean, those are just bricks. Though I must say there are an awful lot of them. I don't know—" She turned to Dad. "Maybe grass would be more welcoming here in front. Less formal, kind of."

"Well, it's a formal-type house, Pat," Dad told her. "Plenty of grass to keep up out back. Anyway, I sort of like the courtyard effect."

"I know," Sean said. "The picture. It's like that picture in one of our books. Remember, Molly?" Molly shook her head. "The book about . . . I can't remember exactly, but some book we had when we were little. There was a fat lady and a dwarf, and it was *scary*."

"That's enough, Sean," Dad said sternly, the way he did when he thought Sean was getting carried away—"being dramatic," Mom called it. "There's nothing scary here. No fat ladies, and certainly no dwarfs." He laughed. "I wish the Warrens could hear that one." The Warrens were the people that owned the house, Molly knew. "Anyhow, just wait'll you kids see all the space you'll have to play in. To say nothing of the pool. You can't see that from here, it's around back, but look—see the barn, and the apple orchard down below? And there's a pond too, down in the woods."

Molly strained to see through the slapping windshield wipers.

"Nothing 'foreign' about the barn, Molly," Mom said, turning to smile at her. "A big old-fashioned New England barn, with a loft where you can play on rainy days like today. . . . You're awfully quiet, hon. Don't you like it, really?"

Molly looked back at the front of the house. Between the first and second stories, a creeper made patterns against the stone, wet leaves clinging like tiny flattened hands. Above the rounded top of the front door, a fan of stonework matched the shape of the shallow brick step underneath. The heavy-looking iron door handle had the same curve, and so did the plate of the big knocker. You could see this was a house someone planned, she thought with an unwilling stir of interest, not one that just happened or that got copied from another house. Also, although it was pretty big, it certainly wasn't the mansion Dad had been making it sound like. One thing Molly had already decided, she wasn't going to live in any mansion; she just wasn't the type.

But she still didn't see why they had to move at all.

"It looks kind of dark," she said critically. "Like it would be dark inside, I mean."

"That's just because it's such a dark day," Mom told her. "Anyhow, I think the inside will surprise you, hon. There are lots of big modern windows at the back—that's south, where the sun comes in. And one of the first things we'll do is cut back all those overgrown rhododendrons along this side."

"Better not let Mrs. Warren hear you say that," Dad said with a grin. "I gather they're some special old-time variety they planted way back when."

Sean had moved across the backseat to the other window and was leaning halfway out of it, the hood of his yellow slicker pushed back, trying to see more of the property. "Can't we get out?" he asked. "I want to see down past the barn."

"No," Dad said. "And shut that window, Sean; you're getting soaked." He started the engine. "I told you before, all we were going to do today was drive by. We probably shouldn't even have stopped. Until we have a firm deal, the Warrens are entitled to their privacy."

"Well, and afterward too," Mom said. "I mean, if we let them stay on . . . Do you really think that's such a good idea, Barry?"

"Better than letting the house sit empty until we're ready

to move. And the rent'll help pay for all the work we need to do on the place."

"But it's going to be so strange for them. I mean, after living here for what, forty years or something, to be just tenants in their own house—"

"Listen, these are classy people. I wouldn't worry about them," Dad said, starting to back out of the driveway. "Any cars coming, Molly?"

The rain was coming down harder. "No," Molly said, craning her head. "Yes."

Dad braked. "Also, it's a good deal for them," he told Mom. "Gives them plenty of time to look for another place. Besides, they've only been living in half the house as it is —they're used to having other people around. . . . Okay now?" he asked Molly.

"Couldn't we just take a quick look around the other side, as long as we're here?" Mom said before Molly could answer. Dad was backing up again. Molly saw a white blur coming fast around the curve on the left. "Hey!" Sean yelled.

A horn blared, and Dad stepped down hard on the brake, throwing Molly and Sean forward against the front seat. The white car swerved, straightened, and sped on out of sight. Dad swore. "Idiot! A day like this, driving without lights— You kids okay?"

They nodded. Molly wasn't hurt, but her stomach was thudding as if something had kicked her. She looked at the house, expecting to see the people—the Warrens—come out. But the front door stayed closed, and so did the side door she'd just now noticed, where a brick path led through the rhododendron bushes. Wouldn't they have heard the car horn and the tires squealing? But if they were old, maybe they were deaf too, like Mr. McCarty next door on Hubbard Street.

"That's a bad curve," Dad said, frowning. "I think it's marked, but maybe we could get an extra sign put up— 'Hidden Drive' or 'Watch for Children,' something like that. Sure, I'll speak to Stan Price about it at the next zoning board meeting." He eased the car out onto the road, super- cautiously this time, and backed it around.

"Of course, usually we'd be coming out of the driveway front first," Mom said, trying to sound casual, as if she hadn't been scared too. "The garage is down by the barn," she explained to Molly and Sean. "The main one, anyway. There's a carport on the other side. . . . Let's just pull in there for a second, Barry; it'll give the kids a better idea of the whole place."

As they drove slowly back alongside the hedge, Molly looked up at the roof again and saw a thin swirl of smoke coming from one of the two chimneys, the one on the War- rens' side. Mom had explained how the house had been divided in half, right through the middle, so the Warrens could live in one side and rent out the other. She'd also said there were four fireplaces, and Dad had said yes, and what a waste of hot air that was going to be, they'd better make sure the dampers fit good and tight. But he'd sounded kind of pleased about it. There was only one fireplace in their house on Hubbard Street.

"Hey, look, another front door," Sean said. They were turning into another driveway, a plain cement one that Molly hadn't noticed the first time they drove by. It ran close to the side of the house and ended in an open carport. On the right, beyond a long rail fence all twisted over with vines, was a big field Dad had said belonged to the next-door house, the one whose rooftop you could just see in the distance behind some tall fir trees. "Why do they need two front doors?"

"For the other people," Mom told him. "They needed their own way in, so the Warrens made a separate door for them."

Molly didn't blame Sean for feeling confused. This door looked just like the other one, dark blue with a rounded top, except that it didn't have any fancy stonework over it and the handle was just a plain brass doorknob.

Dad said, "This is the entrance we'll be using, until the Warrens leave."

"What about the other people?" Sean frowned. "Won't they mind?"

"Oh, there aren't any tenants here now," Mom said. "This side of the house is empty."

Molly said, "Are there two living rooms, then?"

She'd sounded more interested than she'd meant to, and Dad gave her a pleased little smile as he said, "In a way, Molly. The one on this side used to be the dining room. That's what it'll be again, once we take the place over and knock down the false walls."

False walls? Molly still couldn't picture it. It seemed like a funny thing to do to a house. Mom had explained that the Warrens didn't need so much space after their children grew up and moved away. Dad said he thought they could also use the rent money. But if that was why, Molly thought, you'd think the Warrens would just have sold the house back then and gone someplace smaller to live.

"Don't you think we could just peek in the windows,

Barry?" Mom said. She'd been watching Molly's face. "The rain's letting up some. And they couldn't see us around on this side."

"Well . . ."

"Yes, let's get out," Sean said, reaching for the door handle. Molly could tell he was ready to make a dash for the carport, where he'd be able to see more of the land in back.

"Wait a minute, Sean." Dad sat drumming his fingers on the steering wheel. "I don't know, Pat—it's trespassing, after all. I wouldn't want to do anything that could screw up the deal. Now, if we'd called first—"

"Oh, Barry, they won't even know we're here," Mom protested. "And even if they did, I'm sure they wouldn't mind our letting the kids take a quick look at the place."

"Well . . ." Dad said again.

Molly swiveled her head around inside the hood of her sweatshirt and gazed out at the sodden, winter-brown grass of the field to show she didn't care whether they got out or not. And she didn't. Whatever the house was like, she didn't want to come live way out here in the middle of nowhere, in a lot of shaggy, overgrown countryside. She was used to the house on Hubbard Street, where things were neighborly and friendly and orderly, with everyone living on lots that they could see just by looking out a window. In fact, she'd never even imagined living anywhere else. But now it seemed that the whole time she'd thought they were all living contentedly together on Hubbard Street, her parents had been wanting to move. They'd always planned on buying a bigger, nicer house someday, they said, looking at Molly in surprise, as if she should have known.

But Molly hadn't known; and all of a sudden it was like

the house on Hubbard Street was just something they'd used up and were ready to throw away, like an envelope you scrunched up and tossed in the wastebasket without a second glance. Even Sean, who'd never lived anywhere else (Molly almost remembered him coming home from the hospital, wrapped up in a blanket, but not quite), didn't seem to mind the idea of leaving Hubbard Street, he was so excited about moving out where there weren't any sidewalks and the mailboxes sat out on posts beside the road.

"Okay," Dad said, making up his mind. "Everybody out. But just for a minute."

"Come on, Molly," Mom said, tying a plastic rain scarf over her curly brown hair. "Tell me what color you think we should paint the dining room."

A dining room, Molly thought, getting slowly out of the car. Would they have to have all their meals in there, instead of in the kitchen like at home? She pulled up her sweatshirt hood and went to press her face against the cold little diamond panes of the end window, thinking it wouldn't look like a dining room now anyway, not if it had couches and living-room stuff in it. But it turned out the room was empty—just a big bare space with a pinky-gray carpet on the floor and a fireplace on the far side. A kind of chain thing hung down from the middle of the ceiling.

"What's that?" she asked, pointing.

"For a chandelier, probably," Mom told her. "I wonder where it went. Maybe they put it in storage. Anyway, it could be a beautiful room, don't you think, Molly?" Molly just shrugged, but Mom didn't seem to notice. "I thought maybe a sort of dark red for the walls . . . or maybe wallpaper would be better, something with a gold stripe in it. . . . Of course, we'll have to get rid of the carpet." She gave a little sigh of pleasure. "Now all we need is a dining-room table and some chairs to go with it. And the family portraits, naturally."

Molly looked at her in alarm but saw she was just teasing. "There's that painting Grammy made," she said, smiling a little in spite of herself. "You know, the one of Grandpa John."

"The 'wanted' poster." Mom agreed with a laugh. Dad always said that was exactly what it looked like, except for being in color and having a pink flamingo in one corner.

"Sure. And let's see, we could put up your school pictures, and my wedding portrait, and the picture of Dad and his high-school baseball team. . . ."

But Molly had stopped smiling. She was feeling sad again, thinking of Grammy getting sick and dying last summer, all the way down there in Florida. Maybe she never really wanted to move to Florida, no matter what Dad said. Maybe she just pined away, Molly thought, remembering a phrase she'd read, far from her real home in Trenton, New Jersey. But she couldn't help remembering, too, that the home in Trenton had been a dark apartment that smelled of other people's breakfasts, and that the last time she'd seen Grammy, she'd had a new frizzy-blond hairdo to go with her tan and was learning yoga and flower arranging and even scuba diving—"Imagine, me in a wet suit!" she'd said with her jolly laugh—in the big pool at her condo village.

Mom had moved along toward the rear of the house, which went back quite a bit farther than Molly had expected, with just regular windows now instead of the fancy crisscross ones. "Come see the breakfast room, Molly," she called.

"Breakfast room!" That was really too much—a separate room just for breakfast?

"That's what Mrs. Elwood called it," Mom said with a grin. Mrs. Elwood was the real-estate lady. "I think the last tenants used it as their dining room. Anyway, Dad and I thought we could make it over into a playroom for you and Sean. It's already got a tile floor, and if we put up some shelves along that wall . . ."

Molly recognized her mother's planning tone of voice and knew she was beginning to make lists in her head. Whenever Mom talked like that, you could be pretty sure that whatever it was was really going to happen. She peered in at the room, which had white walls and a green-speckled floor. It wasn't very big, at least not for a playroom. But of course there would be the barn to play in too, she reminded herself.

"The kitchen's through there," Mom was saying, pointing at an inner door. "We won't be able to see it today because it runs along the back of the house. Anyway, it's kind of weird-looking now, because it's really two kitchens. But once we take down the dividing wall . . . and of course we'll be getting all new fixtures and cabinets, though there's a nice old gas stove Dad thinks maybe we ought to keep. . . ."

Molly had forgotten about being a trespasser. She glanced nervously over her shoulder, but there was nothing to see except their blue Saab all shiny with rain like a giant Easter egg, and the wet field beyond. Maybe Mom had forgotten too, because now she broke off what she was saying to look around and ask sharply, "Where's Sean?"

Dad was standing at the second-to-last window, sketching something on a pad he was holding under the flap of his raincoat. "He was right here a minute ago," he said, raising his head. "Sean!"

"There he is," Molly said, catching a glimpse of Sean's yellow slicker on the far side of the carport. He was jumping up and down in the middle of some tall bushes, trying to see over.

Dad called again, and Sean came racing back, his gray eyes shining beneath his wet blond bangs. "I saw the pool!" he announced. "And there's a statue, and a thing birds drink out of, and a *big* yard." He spread his arms wide. "You can play soccer there," he told Molly. Sean didn't care about sports, only about roaming around, but he knew soccer was Molly's favorite game.

"That's a lawn, not a yard," Dad said severely, though Molly could see he was trying not to smile. "And it's not going to be used for soccer—plenty of room for that down by the orchard. Listen, Sean, didn't I tell you to stay right here with us? What if the Warrens looked out and saw a strange kid wandering around their property?"

"I'm not strange," Sean protested. "Not if I'm going to move here."

"I told you, nothing's definite yet." Dad gave Mom a look and said, "Time we got going," and she nodded. But he didn't move toward the car right away. He said, "I've been thinking about this little room at the corner, Pat, the one that used to be a maid's room. Depending on how the beams run, I bet we could open it up, make it part of the kitchen. You could put a breakfast table down at this end and maybe have a bank of planters under the windows here—you know, sort of a conservatory effect."

"A conservatory, yet! Listen to him," Mom said, winking at Molly. "Well, I'm glad I get to have a breakfast table, at least. Somehow I can't see us eating our cornflakes in state in the dining room. Or maybe you were expecting grilled kidneys, kept warm on the Sheraton sideboard?"

"Sure, in silver dishes," Dad said with a grin, as Sean said, "Ugh! Kidneys!" and Molly asked, "What's a sideboard?" and a woman's voice called out in high, penetrating tones through the rustle of the rain, "Hello? Hello? Who's there, please?"

 TWO

THEY ALL JUMPED. Dad said afterward that he hadn't, but Molly saw him, though he managed to change it into a kind of casual, swinging turn toward the back of the house where the voice had come from.

"Oh, it's you, Mr. Jackson!" A tall, slender woman appeared around the corner, peering at them from under a jacket she was holding over her head to keep the rain off. "Duncan thought he heard voices, but we simply couldn't imagine—"

"Mrs. Warren," Dad said, and cleared his throat. "This is embarrassing. We were just taking the kids out for a Sunday drive and, well, since we happened to be passing—"

"Perfectly natural, I'm sure," the woman said, and came forward along the narrow brick walk, holding out a hand; with the other, she still held up the jacket. "Mrs. Jackson, how delightful to see you again. And the children . . . ?" She raised inquiring dark eyebrows.

Hastily, Mom introduced Molly and Sean, and Mrs. Warren gave their hands a brisk, cold shake. Mom's face had gone all pink, Molly saw, and wondered if her own had too, the way it felt so hot. Mrs. Warren wasn't at all like the white-haired old lady in a flowery dress that Molly had been vaguely picturing. She wore a black turtleneck sweater and slim green-and-gray plaid pants, and her hair was a pale silver-blond color, cut in shining waves close to her narrow head. She had on coral-red lipstick, and there were thin silver hoops in her ears.

"I'm so sorry," Mom said. "We were just leaving. We didn't mean to disturb you."

"Obviously." Mrs. Warren gave a smile that Molly felt was really only half a smile. "But since you have, let's not all stand about in the rain, shall we? I know my husband would love to meet the children. And perhaps they'd like to see a little of the house."

A little more of the house was what she meant, Molly realized uncomfortably. Mom said, "Oh, I don't think—"

"Nonsense, of course you will. We've got a nice fire going in the living room, and I was just about to put the kettle on for tea. Heavens, look at this child here"—she meant Molly—"without even a raincoat! She must be soaked through. Come along, I insist."

Molly waited for Mom to say that she'd told Molly to wear her slicker but Molly wouldn't; also that she wasn't all that wet. But Mrs. Warren had already turned away, and somehow they were all trooping along behind her sheep-ishly, like captives in a game of Prisoner's Base. They ducked under a dripping lilac bush at the corner of the house and came out onto a wide terrace made of bricks—flat, modern ones, not like the little rounded bricks in front. Molly felt somehow as if she shouldn't be looking at anything, but she did sneak a glance at the sweep of lawn Sean had described and at the pool beyond, its white tiles gleaming dully in the rain. For the first time it dawned on her that she might actually be going to live in a house that had a swimming pool.

But maybe it wouldn't work out, now that they'd been caught trespassing. Maybe the Warrens wouldn't want to sell their house to people who would do such a thing. Molly saw the anxious look Mom gave Dad as Mrs. Warren turned toward a pair of glass doors at the far end of the terrace. He shrugged, then squared his shoulders and stepped forward with his best smile to hold the door for Mrs. Warren.

"Duncan, dear, we have company," she called as they all filed inside—all except Sean, who hung back at the last moment. Molly grabbed his hand and pulled him in after her. Then she stood still, staring.

The room was beautiful, long and low-ceilinged. It ran all the way from the front of the house to the back, and it seemed to glow like the inside of a shell with soft, pale colors and glints of metal and the rich sheen of lamplight on polished wood. A small fire flickered brightly in the hearth of a square white-marble fireplace, behind a low brass fender whose burnished feet were shaped like lion's paws. There was a glossy grandfather clock standing tall in its niche, a carved chest with a silver bowl on top, a round table with a rim like the edge of a piecrust, a wide glass-fronted cabinet with plates standing on end to show off all their different designs. At home they had two antiques, a wooden rocker and a little drop-leaf table that Mom was always rubbing with lemon oil. Here everything looked like an antique, Molly thought in awe.

A ruddy-faced man with bright blue eyes and a gray crew cut had pushed himself out of a deep armchair near the fireplace and was coming forward to greet them, moving a bit stiffly. Mrs. Warren said, "Dear, you remember Mr. and Mrs. Jackson. And these are their children, Molly and Sean."

It was a funny way to introduce them, Molly thought, as if they were just any old people instead of the family that might be buying their house. Maybe Mr. Warren was absentminded because of being elderly. But although his shoulders were a bit stooped under his tweed jacket and Molly could see now that the ruddy look came from a network of tiny broken veins in his cheeks, his glance was sharp and his handshake firm and vigorous. "Delighted, delighted," he said. "What a pleasant surprise, to be sure. Molly and Sean . . . are you of Irish descent, then?"

Molly looked at him blankly. Mom said, "Irish? Oh, you mean their names. Funny, I never think about their being Irish, but I guess they are. No, we just liked them as names. . . . Sean, you'd better let me have your slicker; you're dripping all over the rug. And look at your feet!"

"Never mind, that's what Orientals are for," Mrs. Warren said calmly as Sean stared down at his muddy sneakers. The rug was just a little one, quite faded and frayed at the edges, but Molly could tell from Mom's tone that it must be valuable. "Now, what about some hot chocolate for the children? I think I may even have some marshmallows stashed away somewhere."

Dad said quickly, "Oh, please don't go to any trouble, Mrs. Warren."

"Yes, really," Mom said. "We'll only stay a moment."

"Nonsense," Mrs. Warren told them as she had before,

in her light, crisp voice. "It's no trouble at all. And perhaps Duncan could show the children around the house while I'm getting things ready. You'd like that, wouldn't you, children?"

Sean nodded uncertainly, but Molly said, "Yes, we would," quickly, before she thought. Mrs. Warren put her head to one side and smiled down at Molly—a real smile that made wrinkles in the fine, papery skin at the corners of her eyes. Up close, she looked quite a bit older than Molly had thought at first, with little puckers around her mouth that her lipstick didn't quite fill in.

"That's settled, then," she said with a nod, and left the room, refusing Mom's offer of help by saying that she'd never been able to work and talk at the same time.

"Perfect tyrant of a woman," Mr. Warren said with a chuckle, looking after her. "Lived with her for almost fifty years now, and hardly ever managed to get my own way. . . . Well, troops, ready for the grand tour?"

He held out a hand to Sean, who took it after a moment's hesitation. Molly was surprised—usually Sean was shy around new grown-ups.

"Molly, don't you want to take off that sweater?" Mr. Warren asked. "Looks a bit damp to me."

Molly did want to—her sweatshirt felt all heavy and soggy—but remembered the grungy old T-shirt she was wearing underneath it and said quickly, "No, I'm okay."

Maybe Mom remembered it too, because she didn't say anything about Molly catching a cold in wet clothes. In fact, Molly could tell from the slow way she took off her raincoat that Mom herself was wishing she had on something better than her old checked blouse and the denim skirt that was too tight around the middle. Her hair was all messed up, too, from the plastic scarf. Sean and Dad looked okay, but then they always did, maybe because they were both thin. Well, Dad wasn't thin, exactly, because he had lots of muscles, but his clothes always fitted him really neatly and trimly. In his clean khakis and the blue suede-cloth shirt that matched his eyes, his short, dark hair barely ruffled by the rain, he looked just as dressed up as Mr. Warren did in his tweed jacket and flannel pants. The jacket had patches on the elbows, Molly noticed as she followed along behind Sean and Mr. Warren, and wondered why you wouldn't just throw away a jacket after it got holes that big in it. Unless the patches were on purpose, she thought uncertainly.

At the front end of the living room, on the right, a door led into a square, wood-paneled room that Mr. Warren said was the library. This was where the lighted window had been that they'd seen from the driveway, Molly realized, and the side door that opened onto the brick path between the rhododendrons. Two of the walls had bookshelves running all the way from the floor to the ceiling, and another held guns and fishing rods on pegs. A wide stone fireplace took up most of the fourth wall, with a huge stuffed fish mounted above it, all curved over to make it look like it was jumping out of the water.

"Wow!" Sean said. "A marlin!" That was the kind of thing Sean knew about. "Did you catch it?" he asked Mr. Warren.

"Yes, indeed. Used to be quite a sportsman in my day, if I do say so. Awful waste of time and money, when you come right down to it, but a hell of a lot of fun, too."

Molly blinked; her parents never said "hell" in front of them, except when they were mad about something and forgot. But Sean didn't seem to have noticed. He was gazing reverently at the fish, which Molly thought was gross-looking, with a long, ugly snout, besides being dead. At least it wasn't a deer's head, she thought with a shudder, and wondered if Mr. Warren had used any of those guns to shoot down deer.

"Gave me quite a fight, that old fella," Mr. Warren said with a chuckle, shaking his head. While he was telling Sean about it, Molly edged around the room, looking at things. There was a fat dictionary on a stand, just like in a real library, and also a large, faded-looking globe of the world that spun obligingly when she touched it with one finger. A slippery-looking green leather couch faced the fireplace, but you could tell that where the Warrens usually sat was in the two low armchairs turned toward a small TV set in a corner. There was a magazine on the seat of one chair and an afghan tossed over the arm of the other, as if maybe they'd been sitting there earlier. Molly wondered what kinds of programs they watched. The TV looked old, though not as old as the square black typewriter that stood on a big table against the inner wall. Molly had never seen one like it before.

Mr. Warren noticed her looking at it as he finished his fishing story. "The original Underwood, Molly," he said. "Probably a collector's item by now."

Molly said, "Does it work? I mean . . . how do you plug it in?"

He gave a bark of laughter that turned into a coughing fit. "My dear child," he explained when he could speak again, wiping his eyes with a large, clean handkerchief, "it's pre-electric. That is, you *don't* plug it in. It works on good old-fashioned finger power. An antique, as I say—long since obsolete, I'm afraid, like its owner."

Molly didn't know quite what Mr. Warren meant, but she didn't like being laughed at, so she just said, "I take typing at school."

"Indeed? At your age? Well, a useful skill, to be sure, in this plugged-in age. Next step, the computer terminal, eh?"

Before Molly could say that they were already learning computers too, Mr. Warren had turned away and was leading them out of the library, past the piano that stood by the front windows in the living room—a real piano, not the upright kind, with long, curving sides and a lacy wooden music rack—and under a wide archway into the front hall.

"Still have the original slate floor here," he said, nodding at the flat, blue-gray stones under their feet. "Came from the same quarry as the roof slates. But I don't suppose you youngsters are interested in that sort of thing. . . . At any rate, it's quite an old house, you know, two hundred years or so—this part of it, at least. We added on to the back when we bought it."

"Where the regular windows are," Molly said.

"Right." Mr. Warren gave her a sharp little glance of approval. "And we put in the terrace, and so on. . . . Well, now, let's take a look upstairs."

The stairs were broad and shallow, without any carpeting. Mr. Warren climbed them slowly, one hand on the iron railing. Molly looked at the blank, white-painted wall that seemed to be crowding in on their right and realized suddenly why the hall had seemed so sort of dark and closed in—it was missing the archway into the dining room that should have matched the one into the living room. So this was the false wall, she thought, running the palm of her hand over it as she went up the stairs. It looked like an ordinary wall, but she could feel it was made of something light—just thin wood, maybe, without any plaster.

And here in the upstairs hall there must be other doors hidden behind the wall on the right, more rooms than just the two big bedrooms Mr. Warren showed them on the left, with a bathroom in between.

Sean looked troubled as they went into the second bedroom. "Will I have to share with you?" he whispered. He still hadn't figured it out, the dummy. "There's a whole other side, remember?" Molly whispered back, keeping her face turned away from Mr. Warren. Somehow it didn't seem polite to talk about whose room would be whose with him standing right there.

The first bedroom had been full of heavy, dark furniture, with some silver-backed brushes on the dresser and a pair of worn leather slippers beside the bed—Mr. Warren's room, Molly realized now, because this large, airy bedroom at the back that smelled faintly of some tangy, light perfume must be Mrs. Warren's. Her own parents had always shared a room, and so had Grammy and Grandpa John, but maybe they wouldn't have if they'd had more rooms to choose from. Looking at the graceful four-poster bed with its quilted peach-colored spread, at the soft sea-green carpet that exactly matched the green of the tiny flowers scattered over the creamy wallpaper, Molly found herself wondering if maybe this could be her room. Of course, it wouldn't be nearly as beautiful with just her own crummy things in it, she thought, gazing at the satiny wood of the bureau and the matching dressing table that stood beneath a big mirror on the inner wall. But maybe they'd leave the carpet, at least.

Mr. Warren drew them to the rear windows so they could see out over the property on that side—the big red barn, its boards darkened with rain, the bent old apple trees clustered below it, a stone wall, woods. "The pond's down in there," he said, pointing beyond the orchard while they squinted to see through dark threads of rain. "But don't go exploring around it until the weather dries up. That's marshy ground. At this time of year, the mud can be almost as bad as quicksand."

This was the wrong thing to say to Sean, who loved the idea of scary things like quicksand and earthquakes and avalanches; but of course Mr. Warren couldn't know that. To change the subject, Molly pointed at a white-railed platform outside the innermost window and asked, "Is that a deck out there?"

"A deck?" Mr. Warren chuckled. "No, only the kitchen roof, I'm afraid, Molly. The railing's just for looks. Though I suppose you could make it into a 'deck' if you really wanted to."

He made it sound like a dumb idea, but Molly thought how her mother loved to sunbathe, only she got embarrassed to have anyone see her because she thought she was too fat, and how she wouldn't have to worry about that way up here.

As they were leaving the room, Molly brushed against the edge of the bureau scarf, toppling a small photograph frame that stood there. She righted it quickly, relieved to find the glass hadn't broken. It was a double silver frame hinged in the middle, with a color picture on each side of a girl and boy who looked about the same ages as Molly and Sean. The boy was blond like Sean—in fact, he looked quite a bit like Sean, with gray eyes and thick, dark eyelashes. The girl had medium-brown hair and blue eyes, the same as Molly, only her hair was neater and not so floppy and her face wasn't as round.

"Are those your grandchildren?" she asked Mr. Warren.

He didn't answer right away, and Molly bit her lip, remembering how Mom was always saying not to ask personal questions when she'd only just met someone. But maybe Mr. Warren was just thinking about something else, because after a moment he said, "What? Oh yes, my son's children. Taken a number of years ago."

Sean said, "Do they come visit you a lot?"

"No. Not very often. They live a long way away." Mr. Warren seemed to look past the photographs, blinking a little; then he led them on out into the hall.

"We used to go see our grandparents in Florida sometimes," Sean confided as they started back downstairs. "But Grandpa John had to go in a nursing home, and then he died, and after a while Grammy died too." Again Mr. Warren didn't respond. Either he hadn't heard, Molly thought, or he just didn't like thinking about nursing homes and people dying; she wouldn't either, if she was old. "Our other grandparents live *really* far away," Sean went on. "In Hawaii."

"Ah yes. Nice place to retire, that must be."

Molly said, "They didn't retire there, exactly. I mean, they already lived there. Grandad was in the navy," she explained proudly.

"Oh? I served in the navy myself, during the war. World War Two," Mr. Warren added, though Molly could have figured that out for herself. "What was his rank?"

"I'm not sure," she said, uncertain just what a rank was. "He did things with supplies. His name is Walter Prentiss. Did you ever meet him?"

"No, I can't say I did," Mr. Warren said, seeming to lose interest. "Well, now, what else can I show you? I don't expect you're interested in seeing the cellar. . . . Must be almost time for the tea party, in any case."

They were standing in the front hall again, beside a small half-moon table under a mirror with a twisty gold frame. Molly had been hoping Mr. Warren would offer to show them around the empty side of the house. But of course that would have meant going out into the rain, she realized, looking through a diamond-paned window at the wet bricks and dripping bare branches of the narrow front yard.

Sean must have been thinking the same thing, because he asked, "How did they get upstairs—the other people?"

"Other people?" Mr. Warren looked so puzzled that Molly wondered if he sometimes forgot about living in only half of the house. It would be easy enough to do, she thought, with the way they'd fixed it up and with their half alone being as big as a lot of ordinary houses. Then his face cleared. "Oh, there's a back stairway—goes up from the kitchen hall on the other side. Convenient sort of arrangement in the old days. Kept the children out of our hair when we had company, and the weather on the kitchen floor." He gave his dry little chuckle. "Well, now, come along, the kitchen's back this way."

A separate back stairway . . . As they followed Mr. Warren down the wide center hall, Molly saw Sean's eyes brighten at the idea of being able to come and go without anyone's seeing him. She made a bet with herself that if Sean got to choose, he'd take the bedroom on the other side that was nearest the back stairs.

Mr. Warren showed them a small room off the hall that he said Mrs. Warren used as an office—it had a rolltop desk and a chair in it, but also the washer and dryer, Molly noticed—and then paused by a bathroom, saying, "Anyone need this?" Sean did, Molly could tell; she gave him a little push.

While he was inside, she asked Mr. Warren about the fireplaces. "I know there are supposed to be four," she said, "but I only counted three. The one in the living room, the one in the library, and the one in the dining room . . . the other living room, I mean." She felt her cheeks grow hot; she'd as good as told Mr. Warren about peeking in the windows.

But he didn't seem to have noticed. "Fireplaces," he repeated, frowning. "You're quite right, Molly, there are four. Now, let me see. . . . Ah yes, there's one in the master bedroom. That's in the other part of the house." He waved his hand vaguely, as if it were miles away. "Nice having a fire on chilly mornings, especially in the days when we had a maid to bring us that first cup of coffee." Mr. Warren gave his sudden little bark of laughter. "Imagine, Molly, a maid! Must sound practically prehistoric to you. Ah, well. Probably much healthier for people to have to fend for themselves."

Sean came out of the bathroom then and said, "Who's *that*?" pointing at a picture on the wall behind Molly. It was a small, dark painting in a heavy oval frame of a grim-faced woman with scraped-back hair under a frilly white cap.

"That's—let me see—my wife's great-great-great-great Aunt Mercy. I think that's the right number of greats." Mr. Warren winked at Sean, who was looking abashed in case he'd been rude about someone's relative. "Doesn't look too merciful, though, does she? Or maybe she just ate something that disagreed with her."

The family portraits! Molly thought. Farther along was a bigger painting of a florid-faced man wearing a silk scarf bunched up high under his chin and, beyond him, an elegant lady with powdered hair, holding a fan, who looked quite a bit like Mrs. Warren—she had the same dark eyebrows and glinting gray-green eyes in a narrow, long-boned face. The portraits looked kind of crowded here in the hall, Molly thought, as if maybe they really had hung in the dining room to begin with. She wondered what it would be like to eat with all those people looking at you.

"Oh, there you are," Mrs. Warren greeted them brightly as they came into the kitchen. "I was afraid we'd lost you." She was pouring hot water from a kettle into a slender silver pot.

Molly saw what her mother meant about the kitchen's being kind of strange looking. The ceiling seemed too low for the wide double sink under the window, which in turn looked too big for the small refrigerator and the boxy little stove that stood against the inner wall—the false wall, Molly reminded herself. The other half of the kitchen must have gotten the real stove, she thought, the old one Mom had mentioned that belonged with the house, and wondered if it was the kind that stood on legs and had a place to burn trash, like the stove Grammy used to have in New Jersey.

"Duncan, perhaps you'd settle the children at the small table," Mrs. Warren said, leading the way back into the living room through a swinging door. "It's all ready for them. I did manage to find some marshmallows," she told Sean and Molly with a smile. "A bit dried out, but perhaps you won't notice that when they've melted."

The hot chocolate was good, but Molly would have preferred tea if she'd been offered it—she was secretly trying to lose weight. But probably Mrs. Warren would have been afraid she'd drop one of the delicate, thin china cups; probably, too, that was why she and Sean had been put at their own table near the kitchen door, with a cloth on it and mugs to drink out of. Molly didn't blame Mrs. Warren. If she had a beautiful living room like this one, she wouldn't want kids spilling on it or messing it up, either. Then she thought confusedly that maybe this *was* going to be her living room, hers and her family's. Only then, of course, it wouldn't be beautiful, not like it was now.

She tried to hear if the grown-ups were talking about the house, but they didn't seem to be. They were sitting on two small sofas that faced each other on either side of the fireplace, Mom and Dad in one and the Warrens in the other, with a low table in between. While Mrs. Warren leaned forward to pour the tea from a silver pot that was even taller and more elegant than the one for hot water, they talked instead about the town and how it had changed over the years, especially all the big pieces of property that had been broken up. Molly heard Mrs. Warren say to Mom, "My dear, would you believe I used to ride in the field where the Grand Union is now? That was all part of the

Reynolds estate—you know, the lovely old place at the top of Hunter's Hill, the one with the huge copper beeches in front. . . ."

Molly tried a gingersnap from the plate on the table, but it was hard and hurt her braces. Sean was trying to drink his hot chocolate without swallowing his marshmallow—he hated anything that was too sweet—and getting his face all smeary. Molly glared at him and pointed to the cloth napkin folded beside his place. He eyed it doubtfully, then scrubbed his mouth with it. Now the napkin was a mess. They looked at it in dismay, then shrugged and grinned at each other. Molly didn't know why they didn't say anything. Somehow it felt like they shouldn't.

Now Mom had gotten started on one of her favorite topics, special housing for senior citizens. She was on a committee that had been trying to get the town to buy land for it. "The old Butler place is a possibility," she was saying. "Not as ideal as the Hendrickson property near the center that the town voted down, but it's being offered at a fair price—a low price, actually—"

"It's still too expensive," Dad interrupted, shaking his head. "If you people would think in terms of putting up condos rather than apartments, maybe you'd get some votes."

"Sure, and then instead of medium-price housing, we'd have expensive housing—exactly what we have too much of anyway." Mom's brown eyes were snapping; Molly could tell she'd forgotten where she was, and watched her teacup anxiously as she hitched forward on the sofa. "When you think of everything our senior citizens have to offer this town . . ."

Mr. Warren cleared his throat. Molly saw the twinkle in

his eye, but Mom must not have, because she looked flustered and said quickly, "Oh, I didn't mean you! Or—well, of course I did, but—I mean, it's the really elderly we're concerned about, people living on fixed incomes who love the town but just can't afford the taxes anymore. And if they sell out, where can they go? They can't stay in Dayton, that's for sure, not the way things are now. But an apartment complex, with the state paying part of the tab—"

"Actually, I rather prefer the term 'elderly,' don't you, Virginia?" Mr. Warren interrupted mildly, turning to his wife. " 'Senior citizen' always makes me feel I ought to grow a long gray beard and go around dispensing wisdom to all and sundry."

"Yes, hardly your style, Duncan," Mrs. Warren said, setting down her cup with a little click. She gave Mom a cool smile. "I think it's an admirable project, Mrs. Jackson. But of course that sort of mass housing isn't for everyone. We do have friends who've moved away for the reasons you mention, but I'm afraid being herded in with a lot of other 'senior citizens' would hardly have appealed to them."

"Oh, but the kind of thing we have in mind," Mom began—and stopped at a look from Dad. "Well, it's not mass housing in the sense you mean," she said, and gave herself a little shake. "Listen to me, coming on too strong, as usual! And anyhow, look at the time. . . . Children, have you finished? Because if you have, it's time we were on our way."

Mom never called them "children" except when she was nervous or upset. Molly and Sean pushed their chairs back quickly while the Warrens made polite protests and said they should stay longer. But soon they were in their raincoats once more—all except Molly—and shaking hands all around, and Mr. Warren was opening the glass doors again onto the cold, rainy afternoon that smelled of wood smoke from the fire burning in the marble hearth behind them.

"Thank you very much for the hot chocolate," Molly said to Mrs. Warren. "It was delicious, especially the marshmallows." This was in case Mrs. Warren's feelings might be hurt when she found that most of Sean's marshmallow was still at the bottom of his mug.

"Why, you're very welcome, Molly." Mrs. Warren smiled at her. Her eyes moved to Sean, standing beside Molly in the open doorway, and then returned to Molly; for a moment she seemed to catch her breath, and her hand moved to her throat as if the high collar of her black sweater felt too tight all of a sudden. Then she smoothed back the narrow silver bangle she wore on that wrist, inclined her head with another smile, and said, "I hope you'll come back and see us again soon."

Molly nodded, though she felt a bit bewildered. She wasn't just going to be a guest anymore, was she?—not if they were going to buy the house. But the Warrens hadn't said anything at all about moving, she realized, not one word the whole time. Maybe they'd changed their minds and decided to stay, after all. It was hard to imagine them living anywhere else, Molly thought as she plodded back across the terrace behind her mother and Sean, her head ducked down against the rain, almost as hard as imagining her own family living anyplace but Hubbard Street. Even if you met the Warrens out somewhere ordinary, like at the supermarket or in the dentist's waiting room looking at magazines, you'd know they had a beautiful, special place to go home to—just as anyone meeting Molly's parents would know they lived in a plain, everyday kind of house with a street number over the front door and tan carpeting going up the stairs and a playroom in the basement with a workbench at one end and a washer-dryer at the other.

But when Dad joined them in the car a few minutes later, he had a big grin on his face. "Well, that couldn't have worked out better," he said as he slid in behind the wheel. "Mr. Warren said he'd be in touch. I figure that means they're definitely going to accept our offer."

"Really? Oh, Barry, that's wonderful! I thought I'd blown it in there," Mom said ruefully. "I still don't know quite what I said wrong, but—"

"Forget it." Dad started the car. "So they're too high and mighty to even consider 'mass housing'—not that I blame them, in a way—I have a feeling they're also hurting for cash. After all, the place has been on the market for a couple of years now. I don't think they can afford to wait until a better offer comes along. And they liked the kids. That helped."

He and Mom started talking about plans for the house, but Molly hardly listened. Out of a troubled silence, she said, "Couldn't they sell their furniture if they need money?"

Mom turned to smile at her. "They do have some beautiful things, don't they, hon?"

Dad said, "Well, it's not quite that simple, Molly. I mean, we're talking about a lot of money. And a place like that is expensive to keep up. Must be ten years since anything was done about those drainpipes," he said to Mom with a frown. "Anyway, the Warrens are doing the sensible thing at their age—selling out and using the money to buy a smaller, more manageable house somewhere. Or a condo, maybe."

"Where will they go?" Sean asked, as if he was having the same trouble as Molly picturing the Warrens living anywhere but in the old stone house.

"Oh—Cape Cod, Arizona." Dad shrugged. "Wherever people like that do go. Or who knows, maybe they'll find something around here."

"*If* they can afford the mortgage," Mom said, and started in again about older people and housing. Dad said with what they'd be paying them, the Warrens could live just about anywhere they liked. Molly wondered about that, though. Dad only acted this happy when he thought he was making a real deal, something she knew he was good at.

Sean had been gazing out the window at the wet fields and woods going by, the houses getting smaller and closer together as they approached the built-up part of town. Now he said in a thoughtful voice, "I liked that house, but I don't see how we could move there." When Mom and Dad turned to look at him, he explained, "Well, the outside is neat, but the inside . . . I mean, what would we put *in* it?"

"Oh, Sean," Mom said, laughing, as if it was a babyish question to ask, though Molly had been wondering the same thing. "We'll buy things for it, hon. Not all at once, but as we go along."

"It won't be fancy stuff like the Warrens have," Dad assured him, "a bunch of antiques you don't dare breathe on. Just ordinary, solid, comfortable furniture that can take a beating over the years."

"Well, we might acquire a *few* antiques in the course of time," Mom said teasingly. "But anyway, Sean, we'll be doing over the whole inside—you know, making everything nice and bright, with lots of fresh paint and new wallpaper. And some of our old things will be fine there too; like Dad's recliner chair will be perfect in the den—that'll be our TV room—and the old couch too, as soon as we can afford to get a new one for the living room. A sectional couch, I thought, Barry, that's such a large room, and maybe one of those big, square coffee tables with the glass tops. . . ."

They had left the blacktop road behind for regular streets with curbs and sidewalks and houses spaced evenly side by side, their picture windows glowing behind drawn curtains in the rainy dusk. As they drove, Molly pondered something else that had been bothering her.

"I think they knew we were there all the time," she said at last.

"Molly—?" She had interrupted her parents' planning talk again.

"The Warrens. When we were outside," she explained. "They aren't deaf, so they could hear that car horn. And they could see our car if they looked out the library window."

"Library," Dad repeated, with a little laugh. "Den to you, kiddo. . . . Well, and so?"

"So—I guess they were deciding what to do about us."

"Hoping we'd go away," Sean said, nodding; and Molly thought maybe he was right.

No one said anything as Dad made the turn onto Hubbard Street, their tires swishing on the wet pavement. There was Amy's house, with her dog, Fluffy, sitting on the porch looking out at the rain, and the Herndons' neatly clipped round bushes, and Mr. McCarty's picket fence that he hadn't gotten around to painting last year because his arthritis hurt too much—and now at last their own square yellow house, homely and familiar and suddenly smaller than it had ever looked before, with the tall bare maple tree in the front yard and the tire swing beneath it glistening black and shiny as licorice in the rain.

Dad stopped the car just short of the garage and gave the yellow house a long, appraising look. For just a moment, Molly found herself looking at it through his eyes, seeing it as just a house, anyone's house . . . someone else's house. He said to Mom, "I'll give Mrs. Elwood a call in the morning, okay?" Mom took a deep breath; then she nodded.

 THREE

"WOW! IT LOOKS *neat*." Liza was sitting on the end of Molly's bed, looking at the real-estate brochure of the Warrens' house. Dad had gotten some extras from Mrs. Elwood to show people. "Did you guys get rich all of a sudden?"

"I don't think so," Molly said, a little uncomfortably. "Well, my father did get promoted at his job—"

"Right, Mom saw his picture in the paper." Liza leaned over to study the photograph of the lawn and swimming pool, her long, cinnamon-colored hair sliding across her face.

"And we sold my grandmother's condo down in Florida—"

"Right," Liza said again. "I bet that was worth plenty, huh?"

Liza was almost a year older than Molly, and a lot more sophisticated. She was only in Molly's grade because of having moved around so much. Her mother had been divorced three times. Now she just had a boyfriend, which Liza said made life a whole lot simpler. The three of them lived in an untidy garage apartment over on Seldridge Avenue. "No upkeep," Liza's mother was always saying. "Isn't it divine?"

"Was your dad supporting her?" Liza asked. "Your grand-mother, I mean. Like giving her money to live on?"

"I guess so."

"Well, see, that's some extra money now too. And then there'll be all the money you'll get from selling this house. . . . Listen, Molly, your whole life is going to change, you know that?" Liza brushed the hair out of her eyes and fixed Molly with an impressive brown-eyed stare.

"Just because of moving?" Molly frowned. She took the brochure from Liza and laid it on her desk. "The pictures make the house look bigger than it is," she said. She was pretty sure that was true, even though it had been almost three weeks now since their visit to the Warrens' house. Certainly it was true of the picture of the Hubbard Street house that Mrs. Elwood had put in the paper. It made the front yard look huge, and somehow you couldn't see the houses on either side at all, not even the corner of Mr. McCarty's fence.

"Moving's just part of it," Liza told her. "See, your dad's getting prestige now. That's when you're important. First you need a bigger house in a good part of town, and then you start upgrading your life-style. Or your parents do, any-way. Your mom will have to entertain a lot—that's giving dinner parties and lunches and things—"

"Lunches!" All Mom ever had for lunch was a peanut-butter-and-jelly sandwich, and usually she didn't even sit down to eat it.

"—and probably she'll change her hairdresser and the stores where she has charge accounts. She'll start playing a lot of tennis, or maybe golf, and work out at a health club —you know, the kind with a sauna, where they do mani-cures and stuff." Before Molly could protest that her mother didn't have a hairdresser, just the same barber who cut Sean's and Molly's hair, also that she didn't like charging things, Liza went on, "And then there's a whole bunch of things your dad will have to do, like coaching Little League and joining the chamber of commerce and raising money for things and making speeches. . . ."

"We don't have Little League here," Molly objected. "Or a whatever you said, a chamber thing. At least I don't think so."

"Yeah, but there'll be stuff *like* that," Liza assured her. "I remember from when Ron had his job with Pentoflex and we lived in Ohio." Ron was her mother's second husband. "It's like part of getting ahead. I mean, the company doesn't say you have to do all those things, but they like it if you do. But don't worry, Molly, your father will probably be good at all that junk. Not like fat old Ron." Liza giggled. "You should have seen him trying to show kids how to slide into second base. Let's see . . . oh yeah, and your mom will have to do some extra stuff too, probably. You know, like —what's it called—volunteer work, that they don't pay people for."

"She already does that," Molly told her. "At the thrift shop. She works there every day, practically."

"Oh, right. That's that kind of weird little store next to the women's services place, isn't it? Well, I don't know." Liza looked thoughtful. "I think maybe it should be some-thing, you know, dressier. Like she should get her picture in the paper wearing a suit and pearls and stuff, alongside all the other ladies that run things."

Molly heard the front doorbell ring, and then voices in the hall downstairs. She picked her old stuffed monkey off the floor, kicked her slippers farther under the bed, and tossed some clothes she'd meant to put in the bathroom hamper into her closet. "People coming to look at the house," she explained.

Liza stood up. "I better go. But anyway, Molly, you should just know what to expect. I don't think *you'll* change too much"—she looked at Molly critically—"but you might. Get snobby and stuck-up and everything, I mean. You'll probably join the country club and have riding lessons and go away to summer camp, but that's okay. Just don't let your parents make you go to private school."

Molly opened her mouth to say they wouldn't, and that if they did she'd run away from home, but Liza was already going down the stairs, edging past Mrs. Elwood, on her way up with a "prospect"—a tired-looking pregnant lady with a little kid in tow.

"How are you today, Molly?" Mrs. Elwood said brightly, leading them into Molly's room. "This is Mrs. Blake and— Tommy, is it? Oh, of course, Teddy. . . . Now, isn't this a charming room for a child? Small, of course, but I think you could just fit twin beds in if you ran them like so, on either side of the window here, where the desk is. And there's quite a good-sized closet. . . ."

Molly flattened herself against the wall, hoping Mrs. Elwood wouldn't open the closet door, but of course she did. The woman just nodded, while the little boy tugged at her skirt, saying he wanted to go home now. Down in the muddy backyard Molly could see a bearded, blond man prowling around with his hands in his pockets—the husband, that must be. He couldn't be very interested in the house if he didn't even come inside, she thought. But at least the wife gave Molly a smile before she followed Mrs. Elwood out of the room, and didn't say things like "That wallpaper would have to go, of course" and "Only one bathroom up here for the four of you?" the way some people did.

They were all tired of having the house on the market, especially Mom. Several people had wanted to buy it right away, but Dad had said their offers weren't high enough. A few nights ago, when he'd turned down another offer he said was too low, Mom had gotten sort of mad at him about it.

"Oh, come on, Barry," she'd said, after he hung up the phone. "What's a few thousand dollars? I'm sick and tired of trying to keep this place presentable, the way it keeps raining all the time. I must have mopped the kitchen floor three times today."

"So don't," he said.

"Don't what?"

"Don't worry about presentable. Listen, Pat, this house is going to sell, whatever it looks like inside, *and* for the price we're asking. It's got everything. Close to schools and shops, quiet street, fenced yard for little kids or pets, reasonable taxes"—he sounded like he was quoting the ad Mrs. Elwood had put in the paper—"and it's in great condition. Except for redecorating, it doesn't need a penny spent on it."

Molly knew that was true. Even in the days when her father was a salesman and had to travel a lot, he'd always found time to keep up with repairs. Now that he was manager of the other salesmen and got to stay home more, he did a lot of what he called puttering. He was good with his hands, careful and neat. Molly was the same way.

"Unlike the Warren house," Mom had said with a sigh. She and Dad had a whole long list of things that needed fixing there.

"Right. And that's where those few thousand bucks are going to come in handy, so don't turn your nose up at them. Another couple of weeks, and people who need to be settled somewhere by midsummer will be happy to pay our price. In fact—"

"No," Mom said firmly. "We're asking a fair price, Barry, and we're *not* going to raise it." She fluffed up a sofa cushion and then straightened tiredly, running a hand through her curly hair, that was getting gray streaks in it again, Molly noticed—time for another Clairol rinse. "Another couple of weeks. . . . I don't know how the Warrens stood it, having their house on the market all that time."

"Well, they put a ridiculous price on it to begin with, Pat. Besides, a place like that isn't everyone's cup of tea. In fact, that's one thing that's been bothering me a little—the resale value."

"Resale! Listen, once we get moved in there, that's *it*. You'll have to carry me out feet first." Mom picked up another cushion, then slung it back down and sat on it. "Okay. No more House Beautiful. Let people use their imaginations, since they're going to want to do everything over anyway. But that doesn't mean letting up on the bed making, kids," she added, eyeing Molly and Sean sternly. "And please keep your rooms picked up enough so people can get in the door. That means you, Sean."

At least she hadn't said anything about closets, Molly thought now, listening to Mrs. Elwood taking the pregnant lady back downstairs. She wondered what Sean's room was like—he'd had all his Lego blocks out on the floor this morning—but decided it wasn't her responsibility. He could clean it up after he came back from Tony's or wherever he was.

She sat down at her desk to write her book report that was due tomorrow, and the real-estate brochure stared back up at her. "Elegant Country Living" it said across the top, and below that, "Spacious old stone house on 3.85 acres in the prestigious Winding Ridge section of Dayton, Connecticut."

Prestigious . . . that word again. Molly frowned, trying to remember if Dad had joined anything lately. All she could think of was the club where he played racquetball on weekends. He said it was a good way to stay in shape. It was true that he had more time for town things now that he was home more, like going to zoning board meetings and helping out with the PTA fair. But that was stuff he wanted to do, not just a way of acting important, like she knew Liza meant. Wasn't it?

As for Mom—well, sure, she was looking forward to having people come to dinner in the Warrens' house, where they could all sit around a table instead of having to eat off their laps, but that would be for fun, not to show off or anything. And even if she did get her hair frosted at a beauty parlor and buy some new clothes, like Dad had been after her to do lately, in a teasing kind of way, that would be to please him, nothing to do with her life-style. Molly certainly couldn't imagine her going to a health club. She was too busy with her volunteer job at the thrift shop and with all the housing-committee meetings, and anyway, she hated exercise except for playing games like softball and volleyball at picnics, and sometimes tennis with three other ladies on the town courts, where they laughed a lot and kept forgetting the score.

If only they could go out to the Warrens' house again, Molly thought, maybe the whole idea of moving wouldn't seem so strange and kind of scary. But her parents had said no, not until after all the papers got signed. And even then, although they'd be spending a lot of time out at the house, fixing up the rooms on the empty side, Molly and Sean were to stay away from the Warrens' part as long as they were still living there. Once the Warrens moved out at the end of June, the false walls would come down and they could start working on the rest of the house. Until then—"Well, they say good fences make good neighbors," Dad said. "The same thing should go for walls, even false ones."

Molly sighed and pushed the real-estate brochure aside. She got a piece of clean notebook paper and hunted through the mug on her desk for the pencil with the sharpest point. Then she paused again, gazing down into the empty yard. The sun had finally broken through the clouds, lighting up the forsythia bush just coming into bloom beside the back porch. The Kemps' TV antenna threw its familiar afternoon shadow between the oil-tank cap that would trip you up if you weren't careful and the big flat rock where Toby, the cat, used to lie on sunny winter days, until Mom started getting asthma from him and they had to give him away. Other shadows gathered in the far corner of the fence, the place where Molly had cut her forehead open once when she and Amy were trying to do pole vaulting with a broom handle, of all the dumb things to do. You could still see the scar above her eyebrow if you knew where to look.

The new people, the ones who bought the house, wouldn't know any of those things, Molly thought suddenly. Their kids would go out to play in the yard, and it would all be new and blank to them, like nothing had ever happened there. The idea made her feel strange—not sad, exactly, but old, as if she'd been alive for a long, long time. She thought about the Warrens, who really were old. When they looked out all the different windows of their house, they must see a whole bunch of things happening that Molly and her family could never even imagine, the way no one would imagine just from looking at the corner of the fence how funny it was at first when Molly went sailing off the broom handle, and then how scary and bloody, with Amy jumping up and down and crying so loud the milkman heard her two blocks away.

If she got the chance, Molly thought, maybe she could ask Mr. and Mrs. Warren enough things about their life to try to keep some of their happenings going on for them at the house. It would be like having a collection of pictures she could store inside her head and bring out to look at from time to time. Or like having a videotape, even, that she could run alongside all the new happenings her family would be adding to the house from their own lives, against the same backdrop of the lawn and woods and barn and orchard, the same afternoon shadows and puddles after it rained.

Molly nodded to herself, feeling better somehow. She picked up her pencil and printed her name and homeroom number carefully at the top of the paper. Mrs. Hooper didn't care what you said in your book report as long as you said it neatly and took up at least half the page. If she got it done fast enough, maybe there'd still be time to go down and kick her soccer ball around in the yard for a while before supper.

*   *   *

It turned out to be the Blakes who bought Molly's house—the pregnant lady with the nice smile and her scowling, bearded husband. Everyone but Molly was surprised when they made an offer, even though they came back to look at the house several times. Mr. Blake never looked at all interested. He just ambled gloomily from room to room, sometimes stopping to prod a baseboard with his toe or to swing a door back and forth as if he were testing the hinges, and he hardly ever spoke except to ask bored-sounding questions about the furnace or the wiring or the plumbing. When he got the answers, he'd just shrug.

But one time Molly saw him outside when he thought no one was looking, standing out front under the big maple tree that was just beginning to uncurl its new leaves. At first she thought he was scowling down at the bare place under the tire swing that she and Sean had made with their feet, though grass wouldn't grow there anyway because of all the roots. Then she saw the curve of his mouth in his blond beard and realized he wasn't scowling at all, he was smiling; she saw him punch the tire swing with his fist and then punch the fist into his other hand and spin around to look up at the house with bright eyes, looking like a kid that was getting what he really wanted for Christmas and could still hardly believe it. The next moment, Mrs. Elwood came around the corner of the house, and his face closed down again. His hands went back into his pockets, his shoulders slouched, and he looked as sulky and critical as ever.

The whole business of buying and selling houses was like a game, Molly decided, the kind where you can't let your face give away the cards you have in your hand. Maybe that was why the Warrens had acted so polite and kind of indifferent that day, treating them like guests they might never see again. Anyway, Dad was just as cool as Mr. Blake. When people came back on weekends for a second or third look at the house, he'd just nod at them pleasantly and go on with whatever he was doing, like he didn't much care if he ever sold the house or not. Even after Mrs. Elwood told them the Blakes were really interested, he kept up his casual, take-it-or-leave-it attitude. And whenever he thought Mom was getting too friendly with Mrs. Blake—Mom wasn't good at the game at all, Molly could see that—he'd give her a sharp look and she'd suddenly find it was time to start a load of laundry or put the roast in the oven. It was like she'd for-gotten whose side she was on.

But all that changed after the Blakes made their offer, which wasn't quite the price Dad was asking, but almost. They came over for Sunday-afternoon drinks—without Mrs. Elwood for once—and everyone laughed and joked a lot. Molly had to watch the little boy while Mom showed Mrs. Blake things like the tricky burner on the stove you had to hit with the side of your hand to make it stay on and the washtub in the basement that had the faucets on wrong, so that hot was really cold and vice versa.

Now that Mrs. Blake could finally let it show, Molly could see she was almost as excited about the house on Hubbard Street as Mom was about the Warrens' house. When she went upstairs—slowly, because of her big stomach—her face got that same pleased, inward look that Mom's got whenever she started planning about carpets and colors and where to put things. The Blakes didn't have a whole lot of money, Molly decided, because when Mom said she'd sell them Sean's beat-up youth bed and matching dresser that had been Molly's to begin with, Mrs. Blake accepted right away.

Sean didn't care about his bed, but he was disappointed that the Blakes' kid was so little. "I was going to tell him stuff," he said, after they'd left.

"Stuff?" Dad looked amused. He was in one of his smiling, charged-up moods, pacing around the living room while Mom finished getting supper ready, his blue eyes practically shooting sparks.

"You know. Like about the Habermans' dog—how he'll stop growling at you if you just say 'Good boy, Rolf' and don't act scared. He will, too," Sean said, as if someone had challenged him. "And how Mr. McCarty can hear you okay if you talk real loud into his left ear. Not his right ear, his left. There's a lot of stuff you need to know about. But a little kid like that—he wouldn't even remember."

"Probably not," Dad agreed. "I guess he'll just have to learn things for himself, the way you did." He turned to Molly. "Matter of fact, Teddy's just about the same age you were, Molly, when we moved here from New Jersey. But I don't suppose you remember that." Molly shook her head. Sometimes she thought she did, but she didn't really.

Sean still looked unhappy. Molly thought it was the first time he'd understood, really understood, about moving— how it wasn't just a matter of going to a new place, it was also having to leave an old one behind. "I thought it would be kids our age living here," he said. "Boy, wait'll Mark and Tony find out it's just going to be *babies* moving in."

Molly told him, "Well, I'm glad there won't be anyone my age moving here. What if it was a girl and she was in my class at school and I had to be nice to her and everything?" She stuck her hands in her pockets and went to stand at one of the front windows, nudging aside the oatmeal-colored drapes with sparkly threads in them that Mom was going to leave behind for Mrs. Blake, even though they were quite new, because they wouldn't be right for anywhere in the Warrens' house. It was getting dark out, shadows gathering underneath the snowberry bush where you'd be able to see fireflies later on, when it got to be Daylight Saving Time. "I'd hate for some other girl to be living in my room and doing all the stuff I used to do."

"Hey, *guys*." Dad looked from one to the other of them and spread out his hands, laughing. "What's with the long faces? Listen, you've got to learn to let go! That's what life is all about—change, and moving on. We've had some good years in this house, sure. But now it's someone else's turn —just like it's our turn to start making a whole new life for our family in the Warrens' house."

"I bet they'll feel sad, though," Sean said. "The Warrens."

"Well, sure. It's always hard to leave a place you're used to, even when you know you're making the right move."

"Will the Blakes feel sad, too?"

"They've just been renting some dumpy little apartment, Sean," Dad said, sounding a bit impatient now. "But yes, they'll probably feel kind of sad when the time comes to leave it."

"And the people who'll be moving out of where the Warrens are going . . ." Sean frowned.

"Right. It's sort of like a game of musical chairs," Dad said with a laugh. "Except that everybody gets a chair. Supper almost ready, Pat?" he called.

"Two minutes," Mom called back.

Dad swung back to Molly and Sean. "Look," he said, more gently, "I know you'll miss your pals in the neighborhood here. But they can come visit you whenever you want—spend the weekend, for that matter, with all the room we'll have."

"But that won't be the same," Sean said, and Molly thought that he was right. Then his face brightened. "Hey, could Tony come home on the bus with me after school?" For some reason, Sean loved the idea of riding the school bus instead of just walking to school.

"Sure. And pretty soon you'll have friends in the new neighborhood. I know"—Dad raised a hand—"it doesn't look like a neighborhood to you, but that's just because it's more spread out. Plenty of kids out that way for you to play with. And you'll have the whole summer to get acquainted."

The only person Molly knew of who lived anywhere near the Warrens' house was a girl named Kimberly Reese, who Molly thought of as being stuck-up and horse crazy. She was always talking about her pony and how she was going to be a vet when she grew up, either that or raise racehorses. Also, summer was the worst time to meet new kids. Even though Molly herself wasn't looking forward to having to ride a noisy, smelly old school bus, she knew that was the best way to find out who was around and where they lived.

Mom was calling them into the kitchen for supper. Just as Molly was about to turn away from the window, the streetlights came on along Hubbard Street. When she was a little kid she used to think that was a magic moment, that split second of fading daylight when the lights would flare into soft, pale bloom at the tops of their skinny poles. She used to sit on the porch steps hoping to see it happen, trying not to let herself look away or even blink in case she missed it. But for all her watching, she'd only ever seen the street-lights come on four or maybe five times. And now, when she wasn't even trying . . .

Molly let the curtain fall back into place. She thought about a whole new little family growing up here in this house. It would be like everything starting all over again . . . their turn, as Dad said. She wondered if Mrs. Blake's new baby would be a girl. If it was, maybe Molly could give her the special pillow Grammy had made for her when she was a baby, a little round one with a yellow satin chick on one side, a smiley face on the other, and a frill of lace all around. Molly still kept it on her bed, on top of her regular pillow, but she was getting pretty old for it. Besides, she thought, it might look kind of dumb in Mrs. Warren's room.

FOUR

WHEN MOLLY FINALLY got to go to the house again, the first Saturday after it belonged to them, Mrs. Warren was working out back in the garden. Molly almost didn't recognize her at first, bent over the way she was, and wearing jeans and a wool shirt and a knitted cap pulled down over her ears. It was a sunny, sparkly morning, but still cold in the shade. As Dad eased the station wagon into the carport, Mrs. Warren straightened up and shaded her eyes as if she wasn't quite sure who they were, either. Then she came up the slope toward them, holding a dirt-caked trowel in one gloved hand.

"Isn't it a glorious morning?" she called by way of greeting. "I just couldn't resist getting out into the garden."

They all piled out of the car, including Molly's friend Amy, who had been invited along for the day. Mom introduced her to Mrs. Warren, who said, "How do you do, Amy? Do forgive me for not shaking hands, won't you— I'm simply filthy." Amy just ducked her head; Molly didn't think she knew about shaking hands anyway. "Of course, it's still too early to do much of anything," Mrs. Warren went on, in that way she had of seeming to continue an interesting conversation they'd all been having. "The earth's not really friable yet. Friable—isn't that a lovely word?"

Molly didn't know what it meant, and she didn't think her parents did either, from the way Mom just nodded and smiled and Dad stood jingling his key chain.

"I did just think I'd do some cleaning out around the peonies—they're the Japanese variety, you know, those lovely, pale colors." All at once Mrs. Warren's smile seemed to falter. She gave a strained-sounding little laugh and said, "You know, I simply never thought . . . of course, it's your garden now, isn't it? If you'd rather I kept away—"

"Oh, for heaven's sake," Mom said warmly. "When are we going to find time to garden? Anything you feel like doing is fine with us, isn't it, Barry?"

"Right. Let's just say the garden goes with the lease. On the other hand," Dad added quickly, "don't feel you have to bother with it at all, if it's too much work."

Mrs. Warren seemed to draw herself up a little. Molly noticed how thin she looked, as if she might have lost some weight in the month since Molly had seen her, and pale, too, in the sharp sunlight. But maybe that was partly the way the dark wool cap was drawn tight over the bones of her skull, hiding her elegant hair. Mom had said Mrs. Warren must be in her mid-seventies, a good ten years older than Grammy had been, but Molly hadn't really believed that until now.

"Oh—work," she said, and shrugged. "The garden's always work, I'm afraid. I suppose I just do it automatically, after all these years. And of course I'd hate to see the beds let go."

There was a little silence. Molly looked around for Amy, but she and Sean had already run off to inspect the pool.

"About the pansies, then," Mrs. Warren said, and cleared her throat. "I'd planned to set them out today, in the little round beds in front. They've become rather a tradition here in the spring. But again, I didn't stop to think. Perhaps you'd prefer something else there, Mrs. Jackson—"

"Oh, I'm sure not. I mean, if that's where they do well. . . . And please, let's not be so formal—just call me Pat, won't you?"

"Isn't it early for pansies?" Dad asked. Molly couldn't tell if he was really curious or just being polite.

"Oh, pansies can stand a touch of frost," Mrs. Warren told him. "Not that I think we'll have much more of that this year. As for doing well, that really depends on the summer. Usually I give up on them along about July, and put in something boring like petunias; and then chrysan-themums, of course, in the fall. But in the spring, the pansies are really quite charming there among the old bricks, or so we've always thought."

Petunias were practically the only flowers Mom ever grew. Molly had never thought about their being boring, but suddenly she knew what Mrs. Warren meant. She said shyly, "I like pansies—the way they have those smiley little faces, sort of. And they smell good too."

"Just what I think myself, Molly," Mrs. Warren told her. "Perhaps you can help keep them picked. That's good for them, you know. Perhaps we'll even make a real gardener out of you." The little glint in her eye told Molly she'd caught on that neither Mom or Dad really knew much at all about gardening. Molly found herself hiding a smile.

"Well, we'll leave you to it," Dad said, and gave Mom

a look that said not to let herself get trapped into standing around talking to Mrs. Warren, there was work to be done. "Is Duncan around?" he asked.

"Duncan?" Mrs. Warren seemed a bit surprised at Dad's using Mr. Warren's first name; but after all, Molly thought, Mom had asked to be called Pat. "Why, yes, he's in the library, working on his book. But he's feeling a bit under the weather today, I'm afraid. Is there a question I can answer?"

"Oh, nothing that can't wait," Dad told her, sorting through his bunch of keys. "Ah, here we are." He moved along the driveway to the side front door.

While he was unlocking it, Mom said to Mrs. Warren, "We'll mostly be doing measuring today, and deciding on colors." She fished in her shoulder bag for the paint-sample book. "Later we thought we might have our picnic lunch on the terrace, if it stays sunny."

Mrs. Warren nodded and smiled politely, as if none of this were her concern—Well, it wasn't, was it? Molly thought—and went back to her gardening. As soon as she was out of earshot, Dad said between his teeth, "Really, Pat, you don't have to ask her permission, you know. This is our place now. If we feel like painting the barn purple or ripping out all the fancy flower beds, that's *our* business."

"I know. But as long as the Warrens are still here—"

"Listen, they're going to be here for another couple of months, and we're certainly not going to go tiptoeing around all that time just to spare their feelings. The Warrens are tenants now, not owners, and the sooner they get used to the idea, the better."

Molly said, "We aren't really going to let the garden go, are we?"

"Yes. No. I don't know." Dad gave her a harassed look. "We'll keep the vegetable garden, of course, but all the flower beds . . . That's a lot of extra upkeep, Molly. Just keeping the place trimmed and pruned is going to be a full-time job in itself, especially the way it's been let go."

"Shouldn't you tell her, then?" Molly said, feeling troubled. "Mrs. Warren, I mean. Before she does all the work?"

Mom said, "She'll still be able to enjoy her flowers this year, hon—most of them anyway." She frowned, as if really noticing Molly there for the first time. "Why are you hanging around with us, Molly? Where's Amy?"

"I want to see inside," Molly explained. "This side of the house, I mean."

"Later," Mom told her firmly. "Come on, now, Amy's your guest, remember? There's plenty to explore outside. And I want you to keep an eye on Sean so he doesn't go bothering Mr. Warren."

She followed Dad through the door into the big bare room Molly had glimpsed before through the windows, the one that was to be their dining room . . . that had been the Warrens' dining room too, before they divided up the house. As Molly turned away along the brick walk, she thought that even if the Warrens would be sad to move away, they must at least feel pleased to know the house was going back to the way it was to begin with, with all the rooms used just like they were meant to be.

She squeezed past the lilac bush at the corner, sending a shower of fat dewdrops on herself from the heart-shaped leaves, and emerged onto the wide, sunny terrace. There was some outdoor furniture at the Warrens' end now, she saw, beyond a long wooden planter that hadn't been there before, either, and that divided the terrace neatly in half.

Molly looked around for Sean and Amy but couldn't see them, only their footprints still shimmering in the thick, close-cut grass of the lawn, leading toward the pool.

Dad had said the pool needed work, and now Molly saw what he meant. Some of the tiles were missing and others were chipped, and even through the litter of twigs and leaves that had collected in the deep end, you could see a big crack in one corner. The whole thing would have to be relined with cement, he said; they'd get rid of the tiles. But Molly wondered if maybe they could save some of the pretty, colored ones to put around the edge. These had pictures set into them with little blue and green stones, like mosaics. There was a dolphin, an anchor, a seashell, even a mermaid with trailing hair—

A noise at the far end of the pool made Molly jump. The padlocked door of the little shed beyond the diving board was swinging slowly open; Sean's face grinned out at her through the crack. "Boo!" he said unnecessarily, edging out into the sunlight. "You didn't know I was there, did you? It looks like it's locked, but it's not."

Molly saw now that the padlock wasn't attached to anything but the door itself. "What's in there?" she asked. "Sean, don't go on the diving board, it's dangerous."

"No it's not," he said, but he only bounced up and down twice before backing up again. "Why won't Dad let us have a diving board?" he complained. "Even if this one is too old, we could get a new one."

"I guess it's safer without," Molly said, not adding that Sean didn't know how to dive anyway; in fact, all he knew how to do was the dog paddle. Their parents were already making rules for the pool: only one guest at a time, no running, no ducking, and don't ever set foot near it unless there's an adult around.

"Where's Amy?" she asked.

"I don't know. I'm gonna go see the barn now," Sean told her, and raced away before Molly could tell him about not bothering Mr. Warren. She didn't think he would anyway; he was too excited about exploring.

Molly looked inside the shed, thinking it might have pool furniture in it that they'd be buying from the Warrens. But it was empty, just bare dark boards and cobwebs and a faint smell of chlorine. A stiff old towel hung from a nail, and there was cracked red Frisbee in one corner with a piece out of it, like a bite.

She tried to imagine Mr. and Mrs. Warren playing Frisbee, but couldn't, not even when they were younger. The grandchildren, it must have been, the last time they were here. As Molly closed the shed door and turned away, a feeling of sadness dipped over her suddenly like the shadow of a bird's wing. She remembered her idea of trying to keep things going for the Warrens so that all the old happenings wouldn't get lost. Squeezing her eyes shut, Molly made a picture in her mind of the boy and girl sailing the red Frisbee across the lawn on a sunny day like this one. Maybe their parents would be playing too. They would run and whirl and stretch, laughing and calling out to each other. The boy would catch the Frisbee wrong and hurt his fingers. "Ow!" he'd say, putting his fingers in his mouth. . . .

"Molly!" Mom was calling to her from an upstairs window. "I think I see Amy down by the woods. —Molly? are you all right?"

Molly blinked and nodded, coming back to herself. She

turned to look where Mom was pointing. Beyond the pool the ground sloped down, and it wasn't lawn anymore, just rough grass that ended at a stone wall, with the trees pressing up on the other side. It was shadowy there, but after a moment Molly made out Amy's dandelion-fluff head and saw she was hunched over with her hands on her knees, looking at something.

"Shh!" she said as Molly joined her. "A chipmunk. . . . Oh, it's the cutest thing I ever *saw*." Amy thought all animals were cute, even snakes. Molly was just as glad it wasn't a snake. "It went back inside the wall," Amy breathed. "Do you think maybe it has a nest in there? With eensy-weensy little chipmunk babies?"

Molly could see that Amy was ready to spend the next hour waiting for the chipmunk to come out again. She decided to give it a minute—in fact, she even counted to sixty—and then said, "Come on, Amy, there's lots of other stuff to see."

"Oh, Molly." Amy's soft blue eyes were reproachful. "Now you've probably scared it away."

"Listen, Amy, you can come over and look at chipmunks all you want after we move in. I haven't even seen the pond yet, or the barn."

"The barn! Oh, wow. Do they still have animals, do you think? Maybe there's a horse or cows or . . . I know, a cute little donkey, and we can take turns riding him, like at Caroline Butler's birthday party."

Before Molly could say she was sure there weren't any animals around, let alone any donkeys, Amy was off and running, slapping herself on the rump and neighing—or maybe it was supposed to be braying. Molly felt embarrassed;

Amy could be really babyish sometimes. She looked back up the hill to see if Mrs. Warren was watching. But she was trundling a wheelbarrow out of the garden shed over by the fence and didn't seem to be paying them any attention.

The lower part of the barn turned out to be just a garage now. It had room for three cars, but only one was parked there, an old green Volvo. The rest of the space held tools and hoses and a riding mower that looked even older than the Volvo. But around back, a high chain-link fence made an L-shaped enclosure that did look as if it had been used for animals of some kind. Amy said horses, but Molly didn't think the fence looked like the right kind for horses. Anyway, you could tell that the paddock, or whatever it was, hadn't been used for a long time. The grass was tall inside it, and the door of the lean-to shed in one corner was hanging from one hinge.

"You could fix it up," Amy said hopefully. "If your parents won't let you get a donkey or a pony, you could have . . . well, rabbits, maybe, or ducks. Or goats. Hey, what about a goat?"

Molly shook her head. "My mom's allergic, remember?"

"Oh yeah." Amy thought about this as they returned to the driveway. It was more rock than gravel here at the bottom, with deep, muddy ruts in it. "Couldn't she get shots for it? My cousin has allergies, and he goes to the doctor every Saturday to have a shot."

But Mom wouldn't want to do that, Molly thought, even if it would work. On the other hand, if she had a pet that always stayed outside—if she was careful to wash her hands every time after she played with it, and maybe even change her clothes too . . .

Thinking about this, Molly almost missed the stone steps leading to the upper part of the barn, beyond a trash area with a latticed fence—wide granite slabs sunk in the grass, with Sean's muddy footprints drying on them. She climbed them and pushed through a narrow door into a dim, high-ceilinged space that smelled musty but also faintly sweet, as if there might still be some hay in the loft that stretched overhead like half of a second floor.

"What's that?" Amy said behind her, pointing at a bulky white mass glimmering against the far wall. "Ooh, Molly, it's spooky in here."

"Oh, Amy, don't be dumb," Molly said, but she crossed the splintery plank floor cautiously in case Sean might still be in here, waiting to jump out at her from one of the shadowy corners. "It's just a bunch of furniture—see?" She lifted the corner of a sheet to expose a glossy, curved table leg, and dropped it again.

This must be some of the stuff from the empty side of the house, she thought, and decided she and Sean had better not play in here much until it got moved out; they might wreck something.

"It's so dark in here," Amy complained. "Can't we open that door?"

She meant the big door in the wall that faced the road. It was the sliding kind, but it didn't slide easily. They tugged and pushed and finally managed to drag it open a few feet. Weeds and brambles were caught in the metal runner, growing right up through the cracked cement of the ramp outside. You could see where a track had once curved down from the ramp to the driveway, but it was all overgrown now.

At least they could see a little better to climb the rickety-looking ladder to the loft. Sure enough, there was some hay up there, but not enough to play in—just some old, grayish, stuck-together clumps. Even after they piled all the clumps in one corner, it wasn't enough to jump in. She'd ask Dad to get them some fresh hay, Molly thought as she followed Amy back down the ladder, a whole big shining heap of it. Only of course it wouldn't come that way, it would come in bales. And first they'd have to clear the way in through the sliding door so a truck could back up to it and unload. . . . Molly was beginning to see what her parents meant about all the work that needed doing around the place.

She told Amy they should close the door again. Amy didn't see why—the barn needed airing out, she said. But Molly worried about the Warrens' furniture; if there was a storm and it rained and blew hard enough, some dampness might get on it. She made Amy help her, but even with both of them shoving, they couldn't get the big door to slide back all the way. Finally Molly decided that leaving it open a crack wouldn't hurt anything, and they went back outside by the narrow side door.

It felt good to be out in the sunlight again, even though a sharp little breeze had come up, rustling the crisp yellow heads of the daffodils planted along the house side of the driveway. They raced each other down to the orchard, which was really just eight or nine twisty old apple trees spaced out in a small, square meadow below the garage part of the barn. The ground was pretty flat here, but Molly couldn't see where there'd be room for playing soccer like Dad had said, not unless you cut some of the trees down. You could practice dribbling, of course, zigzagging among the trunks, but even then you'd have to rake up all the apples first.

Molly heard a shout behind her. She turned to see Mr.

Warren standing at the end of the brick walk outside the library door. Even at a distance, she could see that his face was red and angry looking. He shouted again, and seemed to be pointing at something beyond her. Molly looked, but all she saw was Amy swinging by her hands from the lower limb of one of the apple trees. Now Amy dropped to the grass, backed up, and made a running leap at the branch, hauling herself up so that she was draped over it on her stomach, her feet kicking the air.

"Stop that! Tell that child to stop!" Mr. Warren was limping rapidly down the driveway.

"Amy," Molly called uncertainly. Amy was hanging from her knees now, her white-blond hair almost trailing in the grass. From her dreamy, upside-down expression, Molly could tell she was playing animals again—pretending to be a sloth, maybe, like they'd studied in their science book, or maybe a jungle python.

"Get out of that tree!" Mr. Warren called, coming up behind Molly. He was actually shaking his fist, Molly saw in alarm.

Amy hitched herself up to a sitting position on the branch and looked over her shoulder. Then she shrugged and dropped down to the grass.

Molly turned back to Mr. Warren. His face scared her, it was so different from the friendly, humorous face she remembered. He was breathing hard, and his red cheeks were shiny with sweat.

"Isn't it safe?" she asked.

"Safe? Of course it's not safe! Oh, not for the child, for the tree. That tree"—Mr. Warren pointed with a trembling finger—"that tree has been hit by lightning at least three

times, to my certain knowledge. It's a miracle it's still standing. The *buds* are a miracle. Take a good look and you'll see
the trunk's split almost in half. I tried bracing it, but the
cable wouldn't hold. . . ."

Suddenly his shoulders sagged, and his blue eyes stared
past Molly, seeming to lose their focus; he shook his head
slowly and turned away.

"I'm sorry," Molly stammered.

"Sorry. Well, yes, I suppose we're all sorry about a number
of things. One more summer," Mr. Warren said heavily,
starting back up the hill. "Doesn't seem like too much to
ask."

Molly hurried after him. "I'm sorry, Mr. Warren," she
said again. "We didn't know. . . . We'll take good care of
the tree, I promise." Actually, it was one of the trees she'd
been thinking they might cut down to make room for soccer,
but if it meant so much to him . . .

"Yes. Well, not to worry," Mr. Warren said, but vaguely,
as if it didn't matter, after all; or as if he'd forgotten what
they'd been talking about. Puzzled, Molly trailed along behind him. Then, as they reached the brick walk, he turned
to look at her closely and said, "Young Molly, is it?" and
smiled, and Molly smelled his breath and knew what the
trouble was. Grandpa John used to act funny, too, when
he'd been drinking whiskey. Now she noticed that Mr. Warren's plaid shirt was buttoned wrong, so the pattern didn't
match up, and also that his short gray hair was sticking up
in little tufts as if maybe he'd forgotten to brush it that
morning. Whiskey made people forget things, Molly knew.

She tried to think of something ordinary to say, so Mr.
Warren wouldn't know she'd noticed and feel embarrassed,

the way Grandpa John used to—or worse, get mad again. She remembered something Mrs. Warren had said earlier. "Are you really writing a book?" she asked. Dad had told them Mr. Warren used to be a stockbroker before he retired; she hadn't known he was an author too.

"A book . . . Ah yes, my distinguished literary effort." He gave a dry little chuckle. "My wife sets great store by that book, or claims to."

"What's it about? Can I read it when it's"—Molly couldn't think of the word—"when it gets printed?"

This time Mr. Warren's laugh sounded more like a real one. "I doubt you'd want to, Molly, even if that day ever comes. It's just a family history. You know what genealogy is?" Molly shook her head. "Well, anyhow, it's pretty dry stuff, all about the Warrens and the Chesneys—that's my wife's family—going back to the year dot."

Molly smiled; she'd never heard that expression before. "You mean like coming over on the *Mayflower*—stuff like that?"

"Oh, a good deal further back than that," Mr. Warren said, reaching to open the library door. Molly was glad to see his hand wasn't shaking anymore. "Ever heard of Charlemagne? Well, never mind. Actually, the Chesneys were a rather interesting family, more so than the Warrens— some Spanish blood mixed in with the French, early on. . . ."

His gaze turned into the room, where Molly could see a pile of papers and some old-looking books on the big table next to the black typewriter. He was already forgetting her, she could tell.

"Well, better be getting back to it, I suppose. Terrible to stay cooped up inside on a day like this, but I've been running a bit of a cold. Perhaps you children could make a little less noise. Hard to concentrate, you know." He seemed to have forgotten all about the apple tree. Giving Molly a polite, vague smile, he shuffled inside and closed the door firmly behind him.

Amy was hovering at the edge of the orchard, waiting for her. "I thought you said he was a *nice* old guy," she complained. "What did I do wrong, anyway?"

Molly explained about the tree but didn't say anything about Mr. Warren's being drunk, if he was. Maybe he'd been drinking the whiskey to make his cold feel better, she thought; maybe the two things together were what Mrs. Warren had meant by saying he was "under the weather." She decided not to say anything to her parents, either. She wasn't quite sure why, except that she knew Mr. Warren had been feeling sad, and somehow that seemed like it should be his own private business.

She told Amy about making less noise, and Amy asked why. It was Molly's house now, she should be able to do whatever she wanted. Molly repeated what Dad had said about how the Warrens were paying them money to live in their half of the house and they shouldn't disturb them any more than they could help. "Maybe we should play some-where else than the orchard," she added.

Amy looked sulky. "You didn't divide up the outdoors, though. I mean, she—the lady—is over on your side, isn't she?"

"That's different," Molly said. Because Mrs. Warren was gardening, she meant. But she hadn't really thought about that. She remembered the planter dividing the terrace in half. Maybe they shouldn't have gone into the barn without asking, if it was part of what the Warrens were paying rent for.

"Molly! Amy!" Mom was calling them from the far end of the terrace to say it was time for lunch.

"Now your mom's making noise," Amy said with a giggle as they headed up across the lawn. Molly found herself wishing she'd invited Liza today instead of Amy. But Liza might have started in again on all that stuff about life-styles. Amy might be sort of dumb, but at least she wasn't interested in things like how big your house was or how much land you owned.

"Where's Sean?" Mom asked as they arrived on the terrace, looking up from the cooler she was unpacking onto an old bench outside the kitchen door, the only piece of furniture at their end.

"I think he was in the barn for a while," Molly said. "Probably he's down in the woods now."

"You mean you haven't seen him all this time?" Mom gave her a sharp look, then called, "Barry, go give Sean a yell, will you?"

Dad came around the side of the house, looking preoccupied. "Where is he?"

"If I knew, I wouldn't be asking you to call him," Mom told him briskly. She handed Amy a tuna sandwich and said, "Do you want milk, Amy, or soda?"

Dad started yelling for Sean, but there wasn't any answer. He walked as far as the pool, cupping his hands around his mouth and calling Sean's name. Molly glared at Amy in case she was going to make another remark about how much noise they were making, but Amy had her mouth full.

Mom said, in the voice she used when she was trying to

sound more casual than she felt, "Molly, I think Mrs. War-ren's around front now. Go ask her if she's seen Sean, would you?"

Molly found Mrs. Warren kneeling on the bricks beside one of the round flower beds, turning over the soil with her trowel. Next to her was a tray of pansy plants in damp little fiber boxes. No, she hadn't seen Sean, but she was sure he couldn't have gotten lost. "At least, I wouldn't think so," she said, sitting back on her heels. "The woods aren't really very deep, you know. And there's a development now on the other side, five or six houses. . . ."

"Maybe he went to look at the pond," Molly said, think-ing aloud. That would have been her own next stop after the apple orchard if it hadn't been for Mr. Warren shouting at her. Then she remembered what Mr. Warren had told them that first day about the wet ground near the pond. "I hope he didn't, though," she added, feeling suddenly anx-ious. "I mean, if there's quicksand and stuff there, like Mr. Warren said—"

"Quicksand? Oh, now, Molly," Mrs. Warren said with a smile. "I'm afraid my husband has a tendency to exaggerate at times. Plain old mud is more like it."

"You can still sink down in mud," Molly said, "especially if you're only little. . . . And Sean might do it on purpose. I mean, to see if he really *could* get stuck." She paused to think about this. "I don't think he'd go *in* the pond, but he might."

Dad overheard this last part as he came around the War-rens' side of the house from the main driveway. He gave Molly a quick, frowning look and yelled for Sean again. Mrs. Warren pushed herself to her feet, holding on to Molly's shoulder to steady herself. "I'm sure there's nothing to worry about," she said. "The pond's only three feet deep at the most, even in the middle." But it seemed to Molly that she had turned an even chalkier white than before, and she didn't let go of Molly's shoulder. "Sean can swim, can't he?"

"The dog paddle," Molly said, nodding. She hadn't been worrying about the water, only the mud, and even that hadn't really scared her until now. But with Dad starting off down the hill at a run and Mrs. Warren's fingers pressing almost painfully into her shoulder, a horror-movie picture came into her mind of Sean's head disappearing into a quaking yellow bog, leaving only a sinister froth of bubbles on its slimy surface. . . . Dad should have a rope, she thought fearfully; or a ladder would be even better—maybe there was one in the garage—

She was about to go running after him when Mom's voice floated up to them from behind the house. "Never mind, Barry! Sean's here."

Mrs. Warren's hand dropped to her side. "Well, so much for that!" she said lightly. "I suppose country living does take some getting used to, for parents at least. We never used to worry if someone didn't turn up for lunch. Time enough to start hunting if they missed dinner." She picked up her trowel. "Now, Molly, before you go find out where Sean's been, tell me what you think about these pansies. Should I put a white one in the middle, do you think, or a purple? I simply can't decide."

 FIVE

WHERE SEAN HAD been, it turned out, was just up the road, at the house on the far side of the field, where he'd made friends with a skinny, dark-haired kid named Jason, who was between Sean and Molly in age. Amy thought Jason was creepy, the way he hung back at the edge of the terrace, shifting his weight from one foot to the other and darting his black eyes around while he wolfed down the extra hard-boiled egg from their picnic lunch and the extra Devil Dog too, even though he'd told Mom he wasn't hungry; but Molly tried to like him, since he was going to be their next-door neighbor. He had two younger sisters and a father who did something in TV. That was about all they found out about him. As soon as they'd finished lunch, Jason said he had to go home. Quick as a flash, he dodged through the carport, slithered between the bottom two rails of the fence, and disappeared from sight in the long grass of the field.

Dad didn't say anything about having been worried about Sean getting in trouble down at the pond, so Molly didn't either. She felt kind of dumb about that anyway, especially later when she and Amy followed the path down there through the woods and found just plain old gunky mud, like Mrs. Warren had said. Even if you got stuck, there were plenty of reeds to grab onto, and rocks you could use as stepping-stones.

Sean had been there exploring, of course, but he hadn't even gone wading because of a big turtle he'd seen sunning itself on one of the rocks. "I think it might have been the snapping kind," he told Molly that night back at Hubbard Street, when they were brushing their teeth before bed. "If it was, maybe Mr. Warren could go shoot it with one of his guns." Molly shuddered, but Sean was all excited about the pond. He talked about how he and Dad were going to stock it with little trout so they could fish them out again when they got bigger, which seemed like a dumb idea to Molly.

Then he said, "Jason says they never let anyone fish there. Or ice-skate either." He paused to scrub his teeth vigorously —going the wrong way, Molly noticed critically, from side to side instead of up and down like you were supposed to. Through a mouthful of toothpaste foam, he added, "Jason's glad the Warrens are moving. He says they're really mean."

Molly stared at him. "They are not," she said. "Sean, you know they're not!"

"That's what Jason says," he insisted. He spat, just missing Molly's hand as she rinsed her own brush under the tap. "He says they're real stuck-up, and they don't like anyone coming on their property. They throw stones at them."

"Oh, Sean, he was just making that up," Molly told him, deciding grimly that Amy had been right about Jason.

"Uh-uh." But Sean thought about it, standing still in his striped pajamas. "Well, maybe not at people. But they threw stones at Jason's dog."

"Maybe it was getting in the garden. You know, in the flowers. But anyway, I don't believe that either." Actually, Molly could imagine Mrs. Warren throwing stones—a stone, anyway—at a dog that was wrecking one of her flower beds that she'd worked so hard on. But it wouldn't be to hit it, just to scare it away.

"And they used to have dogs of their own," Sean went on. "Big, mean dogs that chased people, even little kids."

Like Jason? Molly wondered. Remembering his furtive manner and the practiced way he'd slipped through the fence, she was suddenly willing to bet Jason had spent a lot of his time sneaking around and spying on the Warrens. She wouldn't blame them for siccing a dog on him—not that she believed such a thing had ever happened.

As if he'd caught her thought, Sean said, "That was before Jason lived there, but it's true. His neighbor *said*."

The fenced-in place behind the barn . . . a dog kennel, was that what it had been, way back when? But even if the Warrens had had big dogs, Molly was sure they wouldn't have been mean ones. The fence would have been to keep them from roaming, not to keep them away from people.

She said carefully—if she made Sean mad, he could be really stubborn—"Listen, Sean, I don't think you should believe everything Jason tells you. Especially stuff he says someone else told *him*."

"I know," Sean agreed unexpectedly. He took a big gulp of water, swished it around noisily in his mouth, spat it out, and then repeated the whole process. He hated having any aftertaste of toothpaste in his mouth; he said it was too sweet. When he could speak again, he looked solemnly at Molly in the mirror and said, "Jason's scared of them—the Warrens. But I'm not."

"Well, why would you be?" Molly stared at him in exasperation. "They haven't done anything to us. They've been *nice*. Like when we were trespassing, remember, and they invited us in and gave us hot chocolate and everything?"

"Jason says that was just because they wanted us to buy their house."

"Oh, that's really dumb, Sean! They're still being nice to us, aren't they?"

But as she fitted her toothbrush back into the holder, Molly couldn't help thinking about the way Mr. Warren had acted that morning, yelling and shaking his fist. Of course, she understood now about the apple tree and the whiskey, but she could see how that might have seemed scary to someone else.

Sean didn't answer right away. He looked down at his bare feet. "*She* told me not to go near that birdbath thing," he said in a small voice. "You know, over where those little hedges are."

"Well, sure—the stone's all cracked, didn't you see? If it fell over on you, it could really hurt you."

"It was the *way* she said it," Sean objected.

"Oh, Sean, that's just the way she talks. It doesn't mean she's not being nice."

"Grammy never talked like that."

Now Sean was just being babyish, Molly told herself, though she knew what he meant. Grammy's voice could be sort of loud and rough, and sometimes she'd really yell at you when she got mad, but it never had a cool, bright edge to it like Mrs. Warren's. She said, "Well, Mrs. Warren isn't our grandmother, dummy," and put the cap back on the toothpaste tube.

"Even if she was, I bet she'd still talk that way," Sean said, and padded across the hall to his room.

Molly thought he was probably right. But that didn't mean she wouldn't care about them. She considered telling Sean how upset Mrs. Warren had been when they couldn't find him and were afraid something might have happened to him down at the pond. But she still didn't quite understand about that. There hadn't been anything to worry about; Mrs. Warren had said so herself. Then why had she looked that way?

She got into bed, and then had to get up again to pull the curtain across the window that overlooked the backyard. The Kemps' garage light was still on, and if they forgot to turn it off, it would keep shining into her eyes all night long. That was the kind of thing that annoyed her parents, but Molly didn't really mind; it gave her a friendly feeling, knowing there was a light burning out there in the darkness while she slept. At the Warrens' house, she thought, it would be black dark outside the windows at night—and quiet too, with hardly any cars going by and no one right next door to turn up their TV too loud, the way Mr. McCarty sometimes did. Of course, there would be a moon some nights. And owls, maybe.

Pulling the covers up under her chin, Molly tried to picture which way she'd be facing when she went to sleep in her big new room. Mom was going to get twin beds for it, and bunk beds for Sean's room, so they could have friends sleep over without messing up the guest-room, which was going to be mainly for grown-ups. Having two beds would help take up some of the space, she thought, comparing all the furniture Mrs. Warren had with her own small desk and chair and dresser.

Mom had been surprised by Molly's choice of a room. "I thought sure you'd want this one," she'd said that afternoon, showing Molly the big square bedroom at the back of the house that matched Mrs. Warren's on the other side of the false wall. "Look, Molly, a window seat, just like you've always wanted. And you'd have your own bathroom too—through here, see? It has only a shower, but you could always use the tub in our bathroom."

Actually, Molly had decided recently that taking baths was sort of babyish; she wouldn't mind having just a shower. And it was true she'd always wanted a window seat, one with a long cushion on it. This one was just bare wood on top, with cupboards built in underneath, but you could probably have a cushion made to fit it, she thought—a velvet one, maybe, with little flat buttons snugged down in the tucks.

But she'd hesitated. "Would Sean get to have Mrs. Warren's room, then?"

"Well, yes. Of course we'd do it over for him."

"Couldn't he have Mr. Warren's room—the one in front?"

"That's going to be the guest room, remember? Besides, it's much smaller and doesn't get as much light." Mom was looking at her in a puzzled way. "We'd planned on these nice big rooms at the back for you kids—in fact they're what really sold us on the house."

But that wouldn't be right, Molly had thought. You couldn't give Mrs. Warren's room to a grubby little boy. She'd pictured Sean's room on Hubbard Street, with its clown posters and the ant farm in the corner and all the Lego blocks. If she had Mrs. Warren's room, it wouldn't have to be done over at all. And she'd do her best to keep it neat. If she ever spilled something on the beautiful sea-green carpet or got a black mark on the creamy woodwork, she'd be sure to clean it up right away. For just a moment, Molly found this a daunting thought, but she pushed the feeling away.

"This room is nice," she told her mother, "but I'd still rather have the other one." She looked again at the window seat and its cupboards. "That'll be a good place for all Sean's junk," she said, turning away.

"Well, suit yourself." Mom shrugged. "Actually, it's probably just as well to have Sean on this side of the hall, closer to us, where we can keep an eye on him."

It occurred to Molly now, lying in the familiar semidark-ness of her room on Hubbard Street while a soft spring rain began its mouselike scurry on the roof above her head, that sure enough, Sean was getting the room nearest the back stairs. She grinned to herself, thinking that if Mom wanted to keep an eye on him, she'd better put a lock on the door at the bottom. From there it was just a short dash around the corner and across the kitchen to the back door. If that would still be the back door, the one that opened onto the terrace at their end . . . ? But yes, the Warrens' kitchen had only that swing door into the living room, so the one on the other side must be the real kitchen door, the one that had been there all along.

Molly frowned at the ceiling, trying to put the two kitchens together in her mind to make one big, sunny room, the way it was meant to be. But it was hard to do. The whole time she'd been in the empty side of the house, her gaze had kept bumping up against the false walls, with a feeling like stubbing her toe. And in spite of all the windows Mom and Dad had opened to let the spring sunshine in, the rooms there felt damp and chilly and lifeless, as if no one had talked or laughed or argued in them for a long time. The last tenants had only moved out in January, Molly knew, but somehow it felt like much longer ago than that; it felt like that side of the house had been standing empty for years and years, ever since the last time the Warrens had a fire in the big master bedroom and their children grew up and went away.

It was still raining in the morning, a steady, soaking, late-April rain that mashed down the yellow flowers of the forsythia in the backyard and turned the grass greener almost as you watched. Mom and Dad decided to go out to the house by themselves, without Molly and Sean. The Warrens were going to be away for most of the day, they explained, and this would be a good chance to do some measuring and planning in the rooms on their side. Molly begged to go along—she wanted to see Mrs. Warren's room again, and also the beautiful living room—but Mom said no, she'd just get bored after a while, and arranged to farm her and Sean out for the day, Sean to Tony's and Molly to Liza's.

Molly didn't think she'd be bored, but as she watched Dad check to make sure he had the key to the Warrens' front door, she thought how her parents would probably be looking inside the Warrens' closets today, and lifting up the corners of rugs and moving pictures to see if they'd left marks on the walls—all the things they'd feel funny about doing if the Warrens were around. It wasn't like they'd be doing anything sneaky, exactly, because they'd called the Warrens first to make sure it was okay to go in their side of the house, but somehow Molly thought it might feel that way, a little. She decided she'd just as soon wait to be invited.

At Liza's they had pizza for lunch, and then Liza's mother took them to see a horror movie over in Holbrook while her boyfriend stayed at the garage apartment to watch a baseball game on TV. On the way back, Mrs. Hurst asked Molly a lot of questions about the new house. "Don't turn into a stranger, now, Molly," she said lightly as she let Molly off at the curb on Hubbard Street. "The gracious-living bit," she explained when Molly looked at her blankly. "I mean, my dear, Winding Ridge Road!—Well, anyway, say hi to your mom for me and tell her I hope we can get together for coffee sometime soon. I did stop in at the thrift shop the other day, but I guess I just missed her."

"Well, she hasn't been there as much lately," Molly told her. "She's been busy picking out wallpaper and sinks and stuff like that."

"Oh, don't tell me," Mrs. Hurst said with a laugh. "I've been that route." With a wave, she pulled away from the curb.

Molly went slowly up the front walk. Before she even opened the door she could smell their Sunday roast cooking—a strong, heavy smell on top of the outside air that was all sweet and fresh from the rain. Lamb, she thought it was, and wished she hadn't eaten so much popcorn at the movie. She wasn't supposed to eat it at all, in fact, because of her braces.

As she paused guiltily to check her teeth in the hall mirror, she heard Dad talking on the phone around the corner. He sounded really mad about something, Molly realized, stand-ing still with her slicker half unsnapped. Now he was hang-ing up with a bang, not quite slamming the receiver down, but almost. Before Molly could even say hi to let him know she was home, he'd gone on into the kitchen, where she could hear him saying something angrily to Mom about how the purchase price ought to be adjusted, either that or they should raise the rent, and Mom saying it was too late now, they should have hired a professional builder to check the house over the way Mrs. Elwood suggested, instead of Dad's thinking he could do it himself. . . .

Molly finished hanging her slicker up. She didn't mean to be listening in, but she couldn't really help it, the way the kitchen door was half-open and their voices were raised.

"Okay, okay," Dad said. "So I made a mistake. But people like the Warrens—I just never thought they'd pull some-thing like this."

Mom said, "Maybe they really didn't know about the leak. After all, it's on the other side."

"They knew about it," Dad said grimly. "They just hoped *we* wouldn't until after we'd signed on the dotted line. If it hadn't been raining steadily since last night . . ." He thumped the kitchen table with his fist, so hard the salt shaker fell over. "A whole section of roof to replace—and do you have any idea what slate costs these days?"

Molly gave up pretending she wasn't there. "Where is it?" she asked, going to stand in the doorway. "The leak?"

"Molly—" Mom gave her a distracted look, then made an effort to smile and sound normal. "Hi, hon, how was your day? Did you have fun with Liza?"

"Oh, come on, Pat," Dad said. "It's no big secret, not anymore. In the master bedroom, Molly"—he turned toward her, biting off each word—"there is a large wet patch in the ceiling, over in the corner near the fireplace. We didn't quite have to put buckets out, but give it another six months or so . . ." He gave an angry shrug.

Molly said, "I thought you were just going to be in the Warrens' side of the house today"—which was stupid and had nothing to do with anything, except she remembered that other rainy day when they'd been at the house and Mr. Warren hadn't shown her and Sean around the empty side. Was that on purpose? She said uncertainly, "Well, you didn't tell the Blakes about the washtub. Or the burner on the stove. Not till after, I mean."

"Oh, Molly, that's different." Mom sighed and ran water into a saucepan. "I guess the Warrens just didn't want to spend the money on such a major repair. And probably they thought we'd discover the leak ourselves when we had the house inspected." Dad gave a snort. "Well, we would have, if we'd hired a professional."

"Back to square one," Dad said tightly. He wrenched open the back door and stood staring out at the dripping back yard. "Such *classy* people," he said, and Molly couldn't tell if he was mimicking Mom or himself. "A real gentleman of the old school, that Duncan Warren. Oh yes indeed."

"Barry—" Mom just looked at him for a moment. Then she took a plastic bag of green beans from the refrigerator and dumped them out into a bowl. "If you want another quote," she said, "how about 'all's fair in love, war, and real estate'? Here, Molly, you can help me tail the beans." She plunked a colander on the counter. When Dad still didn't say anything, she said, "Did you ask them about the chandelier? The one that goes in the dining room," she explained to Molly.

"It's packed away somewhere, and besides, it's a 'family piece,' " Dad said, still in that savage, mimicking voice. "They're not sure they really ought to part with it. Which I suppose means they'll sell it to us, but only at a whopping price."

"Well, I'd love to get a look at it," Mom said, as if she hadn't noticed his tone. "I mean, you can't just put any old light fixture there. And as far as price goes, if we had to go out and buy a new chandelier, or rather a new antique chandelier . . ."

"Maybe it's in the barn with all the other stuff," Molly said, picking up a bean. As she spoke, she remembered about the hay and decided she'd ask Dad about that now; it would be a good way to change the subject to all the fun they were going to have at the new house, away from this hard, angry talk about the Warrens that was making her feel sort of sick and knotted up inside.

But before she could say anything, Dad spun around and demanded, "Stuff? What stuff?"

"You know—the furniture. All the . . . tables and things." Molly faltered, realizing she'd said the wrong thing somehow.

"You mean all that furniture's still there?" Molly nodded. "Well, damn it all!" Dad banged the door shut again. His blue eyes were blazing. "They were supposed to have had everything out of that barn by this weekend."

"Barry, calm down." Mom went to him and put a hand on his arm, glancing toward Molly. "The furniture isn't doing us any harm where it is."

"But the agreement—"

"I know. And it was wrong of them; they should have explained, at least. Maybe they had a dealer coming who didn't show, or they were planning to ship it somewhere and the van was delayed—"

"I don't care what they do with it," Dad interrupted furiously, "put it in storage, sell it, chop it up for firewood—just as long as it's out of my barn!"

There was a silence. Molly looked at the bean in her hand and put it down again. She wished Dad hadn't closed the back door. The lamb smell in the kitchen seemed to be crowding up into her head, making it hard to breathe. But she'd just remembered something she thought she'd better mention, even though it might make Dad even madder.

"How would they get it out, though?" When her parents just stared at her, she said uncomfortably, "Well, there's that one little narrow door, but I don't think everything would fit through there. And the big door—" She explained about how the door wouldn't slide because of all the weeds, and how everything was really overgrown outside, not just weeds but whole big bushes . . .

She kept having to swallow as she talked, and when Mom said "Oh, dear, I never even thought of that" and Dad said "Well, that's the Warrens' problem, not ours," their voices seemed to be coming from a long way away. Suddenly she was sweating all over her body and something awful was rising up into her throat—

She made it to the bathroom just in time.

"Oh, hon," Mom said later, when Molly was settled in bed, feeling hollow inside but a whole lot better, "why didn't you tell us you were feeling sick?"

"I didn't know till right then," Molly said. That wasn't quite true, but somehow it had seemed more important to tell her parents about the problem with the barn, so maybe they wouldn't blame the Warrens quite as much for still having the furniture there.

"Well, I hope you aren't coming down with something," Mom said, and felt her forehead. "What did you have to eat today?"

That was the last thing Molly wanted to think about just then, but she told her, and Mom shook her head and said she guessed they didn't have to look much further than that. She went back downstairs to see about dinner. Molly got up and shut the door and opened the window so she wouldn't have to smell the roast lamb anymore. As she lay down again, it occurred to her that now would be a perfect time to begin going on a real diet, like she'd been promising herself she would. If you started out with a stomach that was completely empty and then were very, very careful about what you put in it . . .

She must have dozed, because when she opened her eyes again she could hear the sound of dishes being cleared away and water running in the kitchen below. Now that the day was almost over, the sky was finally clearing. From her pillow Molly could see a broadening band of blue above the treetops, and suddenly the Kemps' TV antenna flashed gold in a long spill of sunlight. She heard Sean out front, making zooming noises as he rode his bike along the sidewalk between their driveway and Mr. McCarty's, and then her father's footsteps coming up the stairs. He opened the door a crack and saw she was awake.

"How you doing, sweetie? Feeling better?" He sat down

on the end of the bed and gave her foot a squeeze through the blanket. "Hey, it's kind of cold in here. You sure you want that window open all the way?"

Molly nodded; she still did. Dad gave a mock shiver and folded his muscular arms across his chest, the hairs on his wrist glinting against the big dial of the watch Mom had given him for his birthday, that told what time it was all over the world. He'd changed into a shirt Molly liked, a yellow knit with a blue alligator on the pocket, and he smelled of aftershave—not too strongly, though.

"Well, you missed a good dinner, but I guess you don't want to hear about that," he said with a grin. "Listen, Molly, love, I'm sorry about all the yelling I did before. Guess that sort of upset you too, along with the stomach. Right?" Molly started to nod again, then changed it into a shrug. "Anyway, I don't want you taking it all too seriously. It's a great house, and we're going to have a wonderful time there. If it needs a new roof—well, it needs a new roof, that's all. So it costs money"—he gave a hollow chuckle that was supposed to make her laugh—"what's a few more measly nickels and dimes?"

Molly didn't feel like smiling. She said, "But the Warrens should have told you about the leak."

"Maybe they did, and I just wasn't paying attention. Any-way, like your mother said, it's all part of the game. It's up to the buyer to know what he's buying. And probably I made the leak sound worse than it is. We could probably live with it for a while if we weren't redecorating. But you can't put fresh paint on a wet wall."

He gazed past Molly for a moment, gnawing his lower lip with his square white teeth. "If I'd taken a better look at that ceiling—if it wasn't so dark in that corner . . . Well, no use crying over spilt milk," he said, and leaned forward to give Molly's foot another squeeze. "As for the business about the furniture, we must have gotten our signals crossed on that somehow. We'll straighten it out, don't worry."

He stood up, smiling down at her. "Okay?"

Molly wanted it to be, but she could tell that he was still mad at the Warrens. She said, "Will we still be friends with them—with the Warrens? I mean, talk to them and be nice to them and everything?"

"Oh, nice . . ." Dad gave a little laugh, shoving his hands in his pockets and swinging around to face the window. "Sure we'll be *nice*, hon. But it's not as though the Warrens are going to be around forever. We'll be polite, just like we are now. As far as you kids are concerned, sure, be as friendly as you like." He shrugged. "Your mom and I are going to be pretty busy anyway—not much time for socializing."

When Molly didn't say anything, he turned back to her with a frown. "Look, Molly, let's get one thing straight. I know it's a confusing situation, and maybe letting the Warrens stay on wasn't such a good idea. But just remember, we're not their guests anymore. If anything, it's the other way around. After all, it's our house now, not theirs."

He glanced at his new watch. "Well, I've got a meeting to get to. Can I bring you up a glass of milk or some crackers before I leave?"

Molly shook her head, telling herself it was much too soon to start feeling hungry again. "Is it for the PTA?" she asked.

"The meeting? No, for the Boys' Club—a new fund-raising drive. I don't know how I get talked into these things, but when they asked me to be on the committee . . ." Dad sighed, and bent down to give her a good-night kiss; but Molly thought he looked pleased about having to go to his meeting, and his step sounded light going back down the stairs.

 SIX

IN SPITE OF what Dad had said, Molly couldn't help wondering how she should act the next time she saw the Warrens, and also how they would act toward her, especially if Dad had yelled at them over the phone the way she was pretty sure he had.

But the Warrens weren't home the next Saturday, when they went out to the house—"House hunting, probably," Dad said, with an indifferent shrug—and on Sunday they had guests, people who arrived in a new white Mercedes and had drinks with the Warrens at their end of the terrace before they all went indoors for lunch. Mrs. Warren wore a yellow silk suit and narrow high-heeled shoes, and her hair looked freshly waved, with little glints in it. Molly didn't see her to speak to. As the visitors were walking back out to their car, the woman put her hand on Mrs. Warren's sleeve and said, "Oh, Virginia, I simply can't *bear* to think of you leaving this lovely place. . . . I meant to ask you— what are the new owners like?"

But Mrs. Warren had caught sight of Molly in the shadows at the far end of the house, where Dad had set her to sandpapering one of the dining-room windowsills; she shook her head at the woman and called out brightly, "Hello, there, Molly, how are you today?" before she turned away. Molly waved, but she didn't think Mrs. Warren saw.

A few days later, Molly got to go out to the house with Mom after school, on such a mild, sunny afternoon she thought for sure Mrs. Warren would be out working in her garden, back in her old clothes. But she wasn't. In fact, the place seemed deserted, silent and still. Nothing stirred except for a slow drift of white petals onto the grass beneath the old pear tree down by the garden shed.

"Looks like no one's home," Mom observed as she unlocked the dining-room front door. She turned back to the car for some books of wallpaper samples she'd brought along and then hesitated, looking over her shoulder at the calm, gray front of the house. "Go down and see if the Warrens' car is in the garage, will you, hon?" she said.

Molly said why didn't they just use the knocker, but Mom said if the Warrens were resting or something, she didn't want to disturb them. "I just thought if they weren't here, we might take a quick look upstairs on that side. I'm still not sure about the wallpaper for the guest room . . . and then there's your room to decide about. . . ."

"But I don't want new wallpaper," Molly began. "I want—"

"Molly, just do as I ask, will you?" Mom was looking tired and harassed these days. She was giving up her job at the thrift shop like Dad had been wanting her to do, but right now that just meant working extra hours to break in the new person; she'd been more in charge there than Molly had realized. Molly shrugged and cut across the lawn until she could see the garage part of the barn. When they could afford it, they were going to heat it and add on some regular garage doors, but for now it was still open at the front, and she could see that it was empty.

Molly's feet dragged as she started back up the slope. She didn't like what Mom wanted to do. It didn't seem right to go into the Warrens' side of the house without asking first, even for a few minutes. Mom might say they were the landlords, after all, and anyway the Warrens wouldn't mind; but Molly thought they would. Mom would, if it was her. In fact, she thought how Mom would hate it if Mrs. Blake came into their house on Hubbard Street when she wasn't there, especially if the beds weren't made or the dishes were still in the sink or something. Not that Mrs. Warren would ever leave her house that way, Molly was pretty sure, but still . . .

She looked up at the house. Dad was still getting esti' mates on fixing the roof, so for now it still made its sharp, clean line against the sky, with the chimneys standing up alert like ears at either end. All around were shaggy trees and bushes just beginning to blur with leaves, but the smooth stone walls of the house stood firm and orderly against their softness. Molly remembered what Dad had said about pruning and trimming, and hoped he wouldn't do too much of it. If you made the outdoors too tidy, she thought, the house might not look right; it might look hard and flat, like a painting of a house, or like a design of one on mosaic tile. . . .

"Molly?" Mom was waiting for her impatiently.

"Their car isn't there. But maybe they didn't both go,"

Molly said, and added, before she even knew she was going to tell a lie, "because I thought I saw someone in the living room just now."

Mom frowned. Maybe to her the house felt as empty and deserted as it did to Molly. But all she said was, well, they'd just have to wait for another time, then, and was Molly really sure she wanted her room left the way it was? Because there was the sweetest blue wallpaper pattern . . .

"Blue wouldn't go with the carpet," Molly said, helping to clear a space for the wallpaper books on the sawhorse table Dad had set up in the dining room. "The carpet's still going to be here, isn't it?" she added anxiously.

"Yes, if we want it. And it *is* in good condition. . . . Well, how about yellow, then? I think that same pattern comes in yellow." Mom started flipping through one of the books. "Then we could do your bedspreads in yellow and white, with white dust ruffles and fluffy white curtains to match—" She looked at Molly's face and sighed. "I know, you like the room the way it is. But hon, it's so . . . well, grown-up for a little girl. I thought you'd want something prettier and more colorful. You know, not quite so plain."

"I don't think it's plain," Molly said. "I think it's . . . elegant."

Mom looked at her thoughtfully for a moment. "Okay, Miss Elegant," she said, and began turning pages again. "Oh, here's the plaid I thought of for Sean's room. What do you think?" Molly thought it was pretty bright, and that she wouldn't want to live in a room with all that happening on the walls, but she didn't quite want to say so. "At least it wouldn't show the dirt," Mom said, and sighed again. "Oh, I don't know, maybe we should have hired a decorator. But they're so expensive, and what with everything else—I don't believe what a can of paint costs these days. . . . Well, let's take the books upstairs; maybe we can get a better idea from there. Give me a hand, will you, Molly? I don't see why they have to make these darn things so heavy."

"At least we'll be saving money on my room," Molly pointed out, dragging one of the wallpaper books off the table and wedging it under one arm. "Not having to do it over, I mean."

"True." Mom looked at her, and then gave her a quick little hug. "Such a solemn face these days, Molly. And the last few nights you haven't been finishing your dessert, I noticed. Your stomach isn't acting up again, is it?"

Molly shook her head. "I guess I just don't get as hungry as I used to," she said. That wasn't quite true, but she still wasn't ready to tell anybody about her diet; she was waiting for it to show. Mom didn't know she'd also been giving away the cookies from her school lunch and buying low-fat milk instead of regular. As she followed along into the little hall that led to the back stairs, Molly gave a surreptitious tug to the waistband of her shorts. They were pretty tight on her, but then, they were last year's shorts. At least they didn't feel any tighter on her now than they had then.

Every day that week was hotter than the one before, so that by Saturday afternoon it felt more like midsummer than the beginning of May. Molly and Sean were given the job of sweeping out the pool, getting it ready for the workmen who were supposed to come next week. The sweeping part was easy, because they could just push everything down to the deep end. But the steps there were too high to reach, so each time they filled the bushel baskets Dad had found in the garden shed, they had to carry them back uphill to the shallow end, and from there to a dumping place way down by the stone wall.

Finally all that was left was a little mound of dirt and twigs that they couldn't get up with just a broom. When Dad came to see how they were doing, Molly said maybe they should ask Mrs. Warren for a dustpan and brush. (She was around, Molly knew, because earlier she'd seen her out cutting some lilacs—not the purple ones that grew at their corner of the house but white ones from a tall bush near the main driveway.) But Dad said that was good enough for now; the workmen would be making a whole new mess anyway when they started chipping the tiles off.

"Nice job, troops," he said, his shadow falling across them as he stood at the edge of the pool. "Now if we can just get the filter system working . . ."

That was another thing the Warrens hadn't told them about—the pool filter being all clogged up. But although he was all grimy and sweaty from crawling around in the cramped little pump house, Dad looked cheerful enough, Molly thought. In fact, he seemed to have gotten over being mad now that he was involved in changing things and fixing them over, the way he liked to do. He'd even hired a couple of high-school boys to take care of the barn door and do some brush clearing up to the road, after Mom said she thought that was really their responsibility now, and any-way, it would make that whole side of the property look a lot neater. "It's the main entrance, after all, Barry," she'd pointed out. Molly didn't know what the Warrens had said about the furniture, only that it was scheduled to be moved out by next weekend for sure.

"I'd say you guys have earned the rest of the afternoon

off," Dad said now. "Just put the baskets back in the shed, okay?" Sean asked if he could go over to Jason's, and Dad said sure, and he raced away. Molly followed more slowly, feeling sticky and thirsty and undecided about what she wanted to do next. She'd brought her soccer ball, but it was kind of hot for kicking a ball around down in the orchard. Besides, the apple trees were starting to bloom now, which made them look pretty and smell good, but also meant lots of bees.

Turning the corner of the garden shed, Molly almost collided with Mrs. Warren, who was coming out. She looked down at the basket in Molly's hand—Sean had just dumped his inside the door—and said, "Those go over in that corner, Molly, if you please." She cleared her throat and added, "You know, until we decide whether or not we're selling the garden tools, I'd appreciate being asked before you borrow something. Bushel baskets aren't easy to come by these days, at least not good, sturdy ones like these."

She spoke a bit stiffly. Molly felt even warmer than she had before, her cheeks burning as she put the baskets with the others neatly stacked in one corner. She started to say that it was Dad who'd taken them, not her, but decided that wouldn't help, not if Mrs. Warren was really annoyed.

But maybe she wasn't, because now she glanced at Molly's flushed face and said with a smile, "Goodness, you do look hot, Molly! I can see you've been working hard. . . . In fact, you look as if you could use a cool drink of something. How about a glass of lemonade? I could do with one myself."

Molly looked at her quickly to see if she really meant it, and decided she did—though Mrs. Warren herself didn't look hot. She was wearing a silky pink shirt and loose white pants, and leather sandals on her bony, long-toed feet. Her lipstick matched the pink of the shirt exactly. Molly reminded herself that Dad had said they could still be friendly if they wanted, and didn't hesitate any longer. She nodded. "That would be nice," she said.

"Good! Come along, then." Mrs. Warren led the way briskly across the lawn to her end of the terrace. "You might want to give those hands a wash," she said as Molly followed her in through the glass doors and around to the left into the kitchen. While Molly was using the bar of soap at the sink, Mrs. Warren took some lemons from the small refrigerator. "Let's do this right, shall we? Real lemonade instead of the frozen kind. You'll find the squeezer in that drawer on your left, Molly."

There was hardly anything in the refrigerator, Molly noticed. Mrs. Warren saw her noticing and said, "I've sent that husband of mine out marketing—*with* a list, which he'll probably either lose or ignore. . . . Here, Molly, I'll let you wrestle with the ice." She handed Molly a heavy metal ice-cube tray that was so cold it almost stuck to her fingers. "The plastic kind work better, I know, but I do loathe plastic. . . . Just run some cool water over it, will you, dear, until it gets unstuck."

Molly didn't mind; it was hot in the kitchen, with no breeze coming in the open window. When the false wall came down, she thought, there'd be three windows to open, counting the one in the maid's room at the end, and of course the back door too.

"We're getting an ice maker with our new refrigerator," she told Mrs. Warren shyly. "I think that'll be neat, only Dad says they don't always work."

"Like most so-called improvements," Mrs. Warren said, squeezing lemons. "Though I must say I wouldn't mind having an electric juicer, with Duncan still insisting on fresh orange juice every morning. But I suppose it's good exercise for old fingers—helps keep arthritis at bay." She looked down at her hands with a grimace. Molly followed her glance, seeing the corded veins on top and the way her rings slid loosely on her thin fingers, with only the big bumps of her knuckles to hold them on. "Oh, I do think one's hands are almost the worst part of growing old, Molly," she said with a sigh. "Perfectly hideous, and nothing whatever to be done about them."

"Is that what Mr. Warren has—arthritis?" Molly asked. "Why he limps, I mean?"

"That? Oh no, that's from an old war wound." Mrs. Warren reached around Molly to wipe her hands on a wet dishrag and then took two tall glasses from a cupboard. "He was in naval intelligence—supposedly sitting behind a desk, but actually leading quite a cloak-and-dagger sort of existence. Thank heaven I didn't know the whole of it at the time. . . . No, we're both in reasonably good shape, I'm happy to say. Now, Molly"—she held a spoon poised—"how much sugar do you like?"

"Well . . ." Molly hesitated. "I *like* a lot, but I guess I'll only have a little. I'm kind of on a diet," she confessed in a rush, surprising herself.

"At your age?" Mrs. Warren smiled, but then gave Molly an appraising look. "You've got some puppy fat, to be sure, Molly, but you'll lose that in the next few years."

Molly didn't tell her that it was this year she cared about because of Andrew Garrison's calling her "butterball" in gym class. Andrew himself was thin and wiry, with red hair and teasing green eyes, and how Molly felt about him was her secret. Instead, while Mrs. Warren finished making the lemonade, she said, "Well, I don't know. My mom is always having to watch her weight. I guess maybe it runs in my family."

"Probably all your mother needs is some regular exercise," Mrs. Warren said briskly. "Tennis, perhaps, or jogging. We get a perfect stream of joggers going by here in the early mornings. . . . Well, now." She handed Molly a frosty glass with a long silver spoon in it and a thin slice of lemon floating on top. "Where would you like to sit, inside or out?"

"Inside, please," Molly said quickly, and added, "I think it would be cooler."

In fact, the long living room did feel quite cool and shady, with its rose-tinted walls and pale, soft colors against the darker frieze of the rhododendron leaves beyond the windows. It smelled good, too, from the big bowl of white lilacs on the piano at the far end. Mrs. Warren chose a high-backed needlepoint chair near one of the open windows and motioned Molly into a small green-velvet armchair nearby. After she'd set out some china coasters on the table between them, she fished a narrow gold lighter from the pocket of her slacks and took a cigarette from a black wooden box on the table.

"You don't mind if I smoke, do you, Molly? I never do when Duncan's around, he had such an excruciating time giving it up, but I do enjoy an occasional cigarette, dreadful habit though it is."

Molly shook her head that she didn't mind, and took a swallow of her lemonade. It was so sour it made her mouth pucker, and she was afraid she'd made a face; but Mrs. Warren was gazing out the window. "We thought of putting in a tennis court here at one time," she said in a musing voice, "down below the pool. But then there would have been all the upkeep and arranging and so on, and actually the country club was quite a lot of fun in those days. It was still small then, before they added the golf course and had to let in a lot of new people in order to pay for it.—Do your parents play tennis, Molly?"

"Well, sort of," Molly said, setting her glass down carefully on the china coaster. "Dad wants my mom to have some lessons from the pro at his club so she can get better."

"Oh? What club is that?" Molly told her, and Mrs. Warren looked blank for a moment. "Oh yes, one of the new places out on Route Seven. So many of them these days, it's hard to keep track. . . . We haven't played much in recent years—well, we dropped the club membership, it simply wasn't our kind of place anymore, and then our dear friends the Tylers, who had a nice old clay court, sold up and moved to a retirement village—but Duncan used to be quite good, played on the Princeton team and even had a national ranking at one time. Of course that was back in the dark ages when tennis was still an amateur sport, not the commercial horror it's become."

She blew a thin stream of smoke and then gave her head a humorous little shake. "But just listen to me, Molly, droning on about old times, which can't possibly be of any interest to you. . . . Now, how did I get on the subject of tennis? Oh yes, we were talking about exercise. I'm delighted to see you're putting the pool back in shape, by the way. I'm afraid we've rather let it go these past few years."

Molly wanted to ask why; didn't they like swimming anymore? Then she thought it might be because they were too old or because Mr. Warren's leg hurt. Instead she told Mrs. Warren about having the pool relined and painted ("Bright blue, I suppose," Mrs. Warren said, nodding; but weren't pools supposed to be blue? Molly wondered) and also about her idea of saving the picture tiles, the ones that weren't too chipped anyway, to put around the edge. "Dad didn't want to at first because it'll cost extra, but then he decided it would make the pool look kind of special."

"What a good idea, Molly," Mrs. Warren said, looking pleased. "I've been hating the thought of having those tiles just thrown away. They were designed for us by an artist friend in New York many years ago." She put out her cigarette in a square marble ashtray and picked up her glass, smiling reminiscently. "Such fun we had, making plans for this place and then coming out on weekends to see what progress had been made . . . precious little, as a matter of fact, until we discovered old Dan Seldridge. He was a carpenter by trade, but he could turn his hand to almost anything. Dan was a great character, too. I remember the summer the well ran dry. . . ."

Molly listened, stirring her lemonade in case there might be a little more sugar on the bottom. When Mrs. Warren paused, she said, "Was that where you lived before? New York City?"

"Yes, for many years. In fact, this was just our summer place until after our youngest child was born. Then the war came along, and what with one thing and another, we decided to give up the old brownstone and live out here the year round."

"A whole house just for summer!" Molly stared. "You must have been rich," she said before she thought, and felt her cheeks start burning again.

But Mrs. Warren just laughed. "No, not rich, Molly—we were never that. Comfortably off, I suppose. And things were cheaper then, especially here in the country. Of course, there weren't many of the amusements there are now. Dayton had just the one movie theater, and except for the Inn, there wasn't a decent restaurant within miles, let alone the kind of shopping mall you're used to. No fast-food places or bowling alleys or video arcades. We had to make our own fun, for the most part." She made a wry face. "But there I go again, rambling on about old times—and old-fogey talk at that! Do forgive me, Molly."

"But I like hearing about old times," Molly said sincerely. "I mean—well, they sort of go with the house. With all your antiques, and . . . you know, all the beautiful things you have." She looked around the room, not knowing quite how to explain what she meant.

"Ah. And do you like beautiful things, Molly?" Mrs. Warren was looking at her curiously. "Oh, I don't mean just *like* them"—she gestured impatiently—"do you think they're . . . important?"

Molly had been feeling sort of dignified and grown-up, sitting here talking to Mrs. Warren while she sipped lemonade from an elegant, tall glass that maybe had been made just for lemonade, and never mind how sour it tasted—that was part of the feeling somehow. Now she was suddenly conscious of her messy hair, of the scab on her knee that was half picked off and of how grubby her bare feet looked against the creamy, faded colors of the rug beneath her chair. But as she looked up into Mrs. Warren's intent gray-green gaze, she found herself saying, "Yes. Yes, I do," in a firm voice that surprised her, because she'd never really thought about it before—about beautiful things being important.

Mrs. Warren nodded. "So do I, Molly. Whether they're useful or not, whether they work or not, whether they're valuable or not, for that matter, they *count* somehow." She sat musing for a moment. Then she leaned forward and took the wooden cigarette box from the table and handed it to Molly. "I saw you looking at this before. See the carving, the elephant and the acacia flowers? It's ebony, brought back from Africa by my grandfather on one of his travels."

Molly stroked the carving with her thumb, enjoying the silky feel of the wood. She nodded shyly at a tall folding screen beyond Mrs. Warren's chair, where long-tailed birds and flowering branches in pale colors made a pattern against honey-colored silk. "Did your grandfather bring that back too?" she asked.

"Yes, but from a different part of the world—Japan. That was quite an adventure in itself; hardly any Westerners traveled to Japan in those days. . . ."

Talking, Mrs. Warren rose from her chair and led Molly on what she called a Cook's Tour of the living room. Everything in it seemed to have come from somewhere else. The piano had been made in Germany and the rugs in China and Turkey and Persia, a long time ago. The big brass bell in its carved wooden stand came from India, the china plates in the glass front cabinet from France, and most of the furniture from England. Molly was beginning to wonder if there was anything American in the room when they came to the grandfather clock, which Mrs. Warren said had been made in Rhode Island about two hundred years ago.

"Why doesn't it run?" Molly asked, touching the glossy

wood of the narrow paneled door in front, where there was a little keyhole with a tiny brass key in it.

"Oh, it just needs some work done on it. 'Just.'" Mrs. Warren made a face. "To the tune of several thousand dollars, I'm afraid. On the other hand, I no longer have to hear it chiming the quarter hours on nights when I can't sleep. Nothing worse than having your insomnia measured out for you right down to the last tick."

Molly wanted to ask why Mrs. Warren couldn't sleep, but of course she didn't. Several thousand dollars just to fix a clock! she thought. Now that she was seeing the room in a brighter light than on that first rainy day, she couldn't help noticing that a lot of the things in it were kind of shabby and beat up. Fabrics had worn thin on the arms of the chairs, sections of fringe were missing from the beautiful rugs, and the piecrust table had a big chip in its fluted rim. But no wonder, if it cost all that much to fix old things. In fact, maybe you'd be better off spending the money on new ones, Molly thought uncertainly, looking at the dent in the side of the copper kindling bucket, even if they wouldn't be as beautiful or as special.

"Where's Sean this afternoon?" Mrs. Warren asked as she returned to her chair. "Not off getting himself lost again, I hope," she added with a smile.

"No, he's just over at Jason's," Molly said, making herself take a big swallow of lemonade. Now that most of the ice had melted, it didn't taste quite so sour.

"Jason? Oh yes, the Chandler boy." Mrs. Warren's tone was cool; Molly could tell she didn't have much use for Jason. "Thank heaven his parents finally got rid of that horrid little dog of his," she added, sitting back and crossing one leg over the other. "It never did more than snap at me, but when it actually took a nip at one of the little girls . . . Well, I can't say I was surprised. I did try to warn them, but"—she shrugged—"people who've had no experience of dogs always seem to think they know better than those who have."

"What happened to it—to the dog?" Molly asked, feeling an unexpected pang of sympathy for Jason.

"Oh, I suppose they had to have it put down," Mrs. Warren said casually. "After all, who'd want a dog that might harm a child? It was an unattractive little beast anyway, always yapping and digging—some terrier blood there, I expect, along with everything else." She saw Molly's expression and gave a little laugh. "Yes, Molly, I confess I'm something of a dog snob. I don't see why they shouldn't be both beautiful *and* well behaved. I used to raise dogs here, you know—collies to begin with, then wolfhounds."

"Wolfhounds?" Molly swallowed a sliver of ice by mistake. "You mean those big, skinny dogs with the long noses? Aren't they kind of scary and—well, fierce?"

"Big, yes. Scary, no. They're the gentlest dogs in the world if they're raised properly. . . . Wait, I've got a picture right here, I think."

She reached over to the top of a bookcase for a framed snapshot that Molly had noticed earlier because it was one of the few photographs in the room. She'd always thought old people liked having lots of pictures around; but maybe Mrs. Warren thought they would make the room too cluttered. In the snapshot, a younger Mrs. Warren, wearing a striped shirtdress and blue sneakers without socks, stood on the lawn between two very large, slender dogs with long white-blond hair that looked as if it had just been brushed. Their narrow faces were a darker color than their coats, and they almost seemed to have eyebrows, black, emphatic ones like Mrs. Warren's. In fact, Molly thought, holding back a sudden giggle, they looked quite a bit like Mrs. Warren.

"Sandy and Tess," Mrs. Warren said fondly. "Champions, both of them. Of course their official names were much grander and fancier. I raised them both from pups, Molly, and their sons and daughters—or rather their grandsons and granddaughters by now—are still winning best-of-breed ribbons in shows all over the country." She took the photograph back from Molly and sat smiling down at it, her face relaxing and losing some of its lines, so that it almost matched the younger face in the picture. "I did most of the training and showing myself. That's hard work, believe me."

Molly had seen a dog show once on cable TV, over at Amy's. She remembered the people holding leashes at arm's length while they ran around in a circle beside their dogs, taking big, bounding steps on tiptoe and looking anxious. Later Amy had tried playing dog show with Fluffy, but Fluffy wouldn't do his part—he just sat in the middle of the family room getting wound up in the leash while Amy bounded around him, until finally her dad came in and said for Pete's sake, why didn't they take the poor dog out for a walk? Molly had thought the dog people were sort of funny looking; but Mrs. Warren wouldn't have looked funny, she thought respectfully. She would have looked dignified, and calm instead of anxious, as if she were sure of winning.

She said, "Why did you stop? I mean why don't you have any dogs now?"

"Oh . . . Sandy died, and then Tess, and what with one

thing and another I hadn't the heart to start in all over again." Mrs. Warren replaced the photograph on top of the bookcase. When she turned back to Molly, the smile had faded from her eyes; but she said brightly, "Perhaps you could have a dog, though, Molly, once you're settled in. I still have some connections in the dog world, and I could probably find you a nice pup—not necessarily a wolfhound," she added with a twinkle. "Probably you could train it to stay on the place, but if you were worried about its roaming, I think the old kennel's still in fairly good shape."

Molly explained about her mother's allergies, and Mrs. Warren said, "Oh, what a pity. Though allergies can be treated, you know. Or perhaps you could have an outdoor pet of some kind."

That was what Amy had said too, but when Molly had asked Dad about it he'd said no way, they weren't taking any chances with her mother's health, and besides, he didn't want a bunch of animals messing up the place.

She told this to Mrs. Warren, adding, "So I guess he's going to tear down the kennel. Then when we get the driveway paved over, they can do around back of the garage too, and he'll put up a basketball net and stuff there."

"A basketball net," Mrs. Warren repeated slowly, leaning back in her chair. "What a good idea. . . . I hadn't realized you were planning to pave the driveway. We've always rather liked the gravel ourselves."

"Well, it's just that much more upkeep," Molly said, repeating Dad's words, except for the part about how many years it must have been since the Warrens got in a fresh load of gravel.

"Yes, of course." Mrs. Warren cleared her throat. "Tell

me, Molly, what other improvements are your parents planning for the place?"

Molly thought. "Well, I guess we're going to take the
carport down." Mrs. Warren nodded. "And there's the
pond—Dad wants to do a lot of clearing out down there
and make it so you can see the pond better from the house.
Then he'll put fish in it."

"So he can go take them out again," Mrs. Warren said.
Molly waited for her to smile, but she didn't. "Well, I
suppose it's all a matter of what you're used to," she said
with a little shrug. Remembering the big, stuffed fish, the
marlin, in the library, Molly thought Mrs. Warren was talking about fishing, but she went on slowly, "It was always
such a lovely, private place, the pond. You could go down
there and feel miles away from everything. . . . I do hope
you'll leave the big willow tree, at least."

Molly hadn't even noticed the willow tree. She said uncertainly, "I think it's mainly getting rid of all the bushes,
because of mosquitoes. Dad says—"

"Yes, I know," Mrs. Warren interrupted, in a voice that
seemed to hold a flash of anger; but when Molly looked at
her, she appeared more tired than anything else, resting her
head against the high back of the chair. "Damp places are
a fine breeding ground for mosquitoes. Never mind that the
prevailing wind tends to keep them away from the house.
Well, that will be a big project, indeed. Any others?"

Molly remembered in time not to tell her about the rhododendrons; Mom and Dad were going to wait until the
Warrens left to trim them back. Instead she told about the
big outdoor fireplace Dad was going to build onto the far
end of the terrace, with stone seats on either side for a

conversation area, and about all the plans for the kitchen, which was going to have white formica counters and a built-in wall freezer and rotisserie and microwave oven.

"We're going to keep that big old stove, though, for our regular cooking," she assured Mrs. Warren, "the one that's over on our side." The stove didn't quite have feet, the way Molly had imagined it, but it was large and solid, with six burners and a special grill for making pancakes. When Mrs. Warren didn't respond right away, she said anxiously, "I guess the stove comes with the house, doesn't it?"

"Oh yes, Molly," Mrs. Warren said, and now Molly thought she did sound tired. "It comes with the house."

"Then there's a whole bunch of stuff my parents are going to do upstairs." Molly frowned, trying to remember. There was the new walk-in closet for the master bedroom, with the old closet being made into part of the bathroom—"Mom's getting a marble vanity for there, and gold carpeting, and a new shower that will be sort of sunk down in, with a sauna light in the ceiling"—and also the sun deck they were going to fix over, with a door leading onto it from Sean's room. Only of course they couldn't start work on that yet, because it (or rather the kitchen roof, as it was now) ran under Mrs. Warren's windows too, in the room that was going to be Molly's.

Mrs. Warren had been gazing out the window while Molly talked, so that Molly wasn't sure if she was really listening; but when Molly came to the part about her room, she turned her head and said, "You're to have my room, Molly? How nice. And how is it to be transformed? Lots of white ruffles, I expect, and powder-blue walls. Or yellow, perhaps. Yes, I think I can see the yellow."

Molly stared, wondering how she knew. "Well, that's what Mom wanted," she said. "But I don't. I like the room just the way it is now, with the beautiful carpet and all the little flowers on the wallpaper. I'm going to have plain curtains, like you have, and that same orange color for my new spreads, if we can find them and they don't cost too much."

"Please, Molly, not orange!—apricot, perhaps, or peach," Mrs. Warren corrected her with a little shudder; but Molly thought she looked pleased. "Yes, I've always liked that carpet too, though I'm afraid you'll find it a bit worn in places. . . . As for the curtains—actually they're pongee silk, and handmade too, so not quite so plain as you suppose— I'll make you a present of them, if you like. Just be sure to tell your mother they have to be cleaned very carefully; otherwise the silk may stretch or shred. The Honeycut Cleaners down in Old Harbor are really the only ones I know of who still understand how to handle old fabrics."

"Really? I mean, can I really have them?" Molly was delighted, though she had a moment's doubt about whether Mom would think the curtains were worth all that trouble—Old Harbor was quite a long drive away, she knew, down on the Sound—instead of being the kind you could just throw in the washer when they got dirty. "Won't you need them where you're going?"

"Oh, I don't think so. They were made for the room, you see."

There was a little silence. Hesitantly, Molly said, "Do you know where you're moving to yet? I mean, did you find another house to buy?"

"No, not yet, Molly." Mrs. Warren stirred in her chair. "Actually, we may decide to rent rather than buy. It seems more practical. Though there's a rather charming little cottage over in Ludbury we've had our eye on that's not on the market yet officially." Ludbury was the next-door town, smaller and more countrified than Dayton. "And of course there are several other possibilities." She gave a shrug. "We'll see."

"A cottage," Molly repeated. "You mean a really little place? But how would you fit all your furniture in?"

"I don't suppose we would," Mrs. Warren told her lightly. "We'll just have to do some picking and choosing when the time comes. Ah, I thought I heard the car," she said, turning her head toward the front hall as the screen door banged open and shut and Mr. Warren's voice announced, "I'm back, dear."

Knowing it was time for her to leave, and realizing too late that she hadn't found out half the stuff she wanted to know, Molly said as she stood up, "Do you think maybe I could look at your pictures sometime, Mrs. Warren?"

"Pictures, Molly?" Mrs. Warren said distractedly as Mr. Warren called from the hallway, "Just wait till you see what I got us for dinner!"

"Of you and your children when they were growing up, and your grandchildren too, and—you know, everything the way it used to be. Like an album," Molly explained.

"Oh. Yes, I see." Mrs. Warren too had risen; she stood smoothing the palms of her hands against her pink shirt, looking down at Molly with a little frown that drew her eyebrows together in a straight, dark line. "Well, I don't really know whether we still have such a thing, Molly. Up in the attic, perhaps . . ."

"But aren't they to keep out?" Molly said, puzzled, remembering the two fat photo albums Grammy always kept on her knickknack shelf, next to the tiny pair of bronzed wrinkled shoes Dad had worn when he was a baby. Now her family had those albums in the bookcase shelf along with their own, though Mom had put the shoes away somewhere, saying they gave her the creeps.

"Yes, of course, depending on how well organized one is," Mrs. Warren said with a little laugh. "But—"

"Swordfish," Mr. Warren said in a triumphant voice, appearing in the kitchen doorway. "Oh, hello, there, Molly—came to tea again, did you? Yes, only six-forty-nine a pound," he said to Mrs. Warren. "Looks nice and fresh, too." He disappeared. Molly could hear the crackling of paper bags as he began unpacking the groceries.

"Oh, dear God," Mrs. Warren said in a whisper, closing her eyes. "I wonder how many pounds he bought. . . ." Raising her voice, she called, "That sounds lovely, Duncan." To Molly she said, "I'll see what I can find, dear," and gave her a bright, vague smile as she moved toward the kitchen.

Quickly, Molly thanked her for the lemonade, though she didn't think Mrs. Warren really heard her. As she let herself out through the glass doors onto the hot glare of the terrace, Mr. Warren was saying in a tone of satisfaction, "Swordfish steak and artichokes—now, they weren't really very expensive, Virginia, it's still the season—and I got some extra butter too, in case you felt like making a hollandaise sauce. A veritable feast, my dear!"

Mrs. Warren's reply sounded almost anguished to Molly. "Oh, Duncan, look at the size of it! . . . Well, I suppose we can cut it in half and put the rest in the freezer, though it's never as good after it's been frozen. Oh, good, you remembered coffee, and the Cooper's marmalade—But what's all this? Duncan, you didn't buy *everything* at the Village Mart, did you? At those prices? I specifically asked you to get the staples at the Safeway, and the lamb chops that were on sale—"

"Yes, well, you know me, never could find my way around a supermarket—great barns of places, and never anyone in sight to answer a civil question. . . ."

Molly went through the kitchen door on her side of the house and got a drink of water to take away the scratchy feeling the lemonade had left in her throat. She could still hear the Warrens' voices faintly on the other side of the false wall, though not what they were saying. She didn't want to anyway—she hated it when grown-ups started arguing and getting mad at each other. Except Mrs. Warren hadn't sounded mad so much as worried, she thought uneasily, as if maybe the money Mr. Warren had spent on the groceries really was more than they could afford. For the first time, too, Mrs. Warren had sounded old, like an ordinary elderly person, with the same harsh note in her voice that Mr. McCarty's got when he opened his oil bill and said how did they expect someone living alone on a pension to pay out that kind of money, he already had the thermostat turned down as low as he could stand it. . . .

But later, when she told her parents about the shabby furniture and the expensive groceries and how she was afraid the Warrens might not really have very much money at all, they just laughed. "Oh, Molly, the Warrens probably don't even notice the furniture anymore," Mom said. "And as for the grocery bill, that's a conversation most husbands and wives have at least once a month. It doesn't mean they're poor."

"But what if they are?" Molly persisted. "I mean, I know we're paying them a lot of money for the house, but—"

"Probably they have bills to pay off," Dad told her, "and

meanwhile they're economizing. Or maybe Mrs. Warren is just naturally thrifty." For a moment he looked grim, and Molly knew he was thinking about the leak the Warrens hadn't had fixed. "But as for being poor in the way you mean, Molly . . ." He shook his head. "No way. People like the Warrens always have something to fall back on. For them, being poor just means not being as comfortably off as they were before. It's not the same thing, believe me."

They all looked at him respectfully. Dad had been really poor when he was growing up, after Grandpa John hurt his back and got laid off from the tomato cannery. Grammy had to go out cleaning other people's houses, and Dad himself had started earning regular money when he was twelve, washing dishes and sweeping floors after school at a restaurant. One of the ladies Grammy worked for used to give her the clothes her son had outgrown, and they weren't even clean; Grammy had to boil them on top of the stove before she'd let Dad wear them. So if he said the Warrens weren't poor, Molly thought, he must be right. Maybe when you were really comfortably off, you didn't have to think about how much things cost, and when you weren't quite so comfortable, you did; that was probably all it was.

SEVEN

AFTER THAT WEEKEND, everything out at the house started getting to be in a real mess. The area around the pool became littered with broken tiles, and there were deep gouges in the lawn where a truck had backed in to deliver the heavy bags of cement. In front, where work had begun on the roof, pieces of slate and roofing paper and nails were scattered over the old bricks, and Molly and Sean were no longer allowed to go barefoot. One of the little round beds of pansies got all squashed from having the end of a ladder stuck in it. Molly did her best to fix it up, picking out the limp petals and broken stems and smoothing the earth around the remaining plants; but the next time she went out to the house, a big chunk of plaster had fallen into the bed and the plants looked brown and dead.

She wondered if Mrs. Warren even noticed. At first, as the flower beds began blooming in rainbow waves of bright spring color, Mrs. Warren was often out tending her garden, wearing a shady straw hat now and a cotton smock like an art teacher's. She seemed to ignore all the mess and confu-

sion, picking her way without comment around the big heap
of stones for the outdoor fireplace that had been dumped on
the grass beside the terrace. She didn't even seem upset the
day Dad and the high-school boys took down the carport
and one of the big wooden posts smashed down across the
end of the long flower bed nearest the fence. They moved
it off right away, but still, Molly saw, a whole group of tall
plants at the back had had their stalks snapped right in two.

"The delphinium," Mrs. Warren said, looking down at
the broken stem Molly brought to show her. "Another few
weeks, Molly, and you'd have seen such shades of blue. . . .
But no, dear, I'm afraid there's nothing to be done, thank
you all the same. With some care, they might still produce
a second bloom in the fall, but . . ." She shrugged. "They're
fussy plants in any case; I doubt whether your mother will
want to bother with them. Oh, please, Molly, don't look so
tragic! A high wind or a hailstorm could have done the same
thing, especially since I hadn't gotten around to staking them
yet. Lovely things, delphinium, but fragile," she said, and
tossed the wilting branch aside onto the compost heap. "A
matter of gardener's luck."

But Molly noticed that after that Mrs. Warren didn't
come over to the flower beds on their side of the property
as much, except to "deadhead"—plucking off the flowers
that had already bloomed. After a while she didn't even do
that very often, so Molly did it instead, though sometimes
it was hard to tell if a flower was just starting to open or
just finishing.

Meanwhile the inside of the house on Molly's side was
getting to be as much of a mess as the outside. Rolls of
wallpaper leaned against the corners, and the baseboards

were lined with paint cans and sanders and strips of molding and bathroom fixtures. She and Sean helped Dad drag the old carpet out of the dining room, exposing a wide-plank floor that Dad was going to sand down and refinish. Upstairs Mom was putting up the plaid wallpaper in Sean's room. She complained that it made her dizzy, trying to match the plaid at the corners. It made Molly dizzy just to look at, but maybe it wouldn't be so bad once Sean's new bunk beds got moved in and covered at least one of the walls.

Sean himself didn't seem to mind, but then he was hardly ever around. He was always over at Jason's, or going off on walks with Mr. Warren, who had given up working on his book while the roof was being fixed. "Like having a flock of woodpeckers camped on top of you," he said, which made Sean laugh; but Molly couldn't help thinking that after all the leak was the Warrens' fault to begin with, and also that the library was at the far end of the house from where the workmen were—maybe Mr. Warren was just getting bored with learning about old families. Anyway, he said Sean should know about things like where the birds' nests were, and the old beaver dam that had helped make the pond, and the place up the road where they'd once turned up a flintlock from a Revolutionary War musket.

"Why just Sean?" Molly grumbled to her mother. "Why not me, too?"

"I'm sure Mr. Warren would be glad to have you along, hon. Just ask him, why don't you?"

Molly felt shy about asking, but she knew Mom wouldn't speak to Mr. Warren for her. She and Dad only ever really talked to the Warrens when they had questions about things like where a certain pipe ran to or where the screens were for the playroom windows. Otherwise they just smiled briefly and said "Hello" and "Beautiful day, isn't it?" and "Well, I guess we're off now"—being polite, as Dad had said.

Anyway, when Molly did ask, Mr. Warren said heartily, "Fine, fine, Molly, by all means join the expedition," so that part was okay. But the walk didn't turn out to be much fun. Mr. Warren had to go slowly because of his leg—he used a cane, only he called it a walking stick—and he kept stopping to point out things that Molly either couldn't see at all, even when she looked through his field glasses, or wasn't interested in, like a certain kind of sparrow or a big gray rock he said had been made by a glacier. The deerflies were bad down in the woods, and Molly kept hearing thunder in the distance and worrying about being under so many trees if there was going to be lightning too. Neither Mr. Warren nor Sean seemed to notice. Sean, who was usually so impatient to be on the move, stayed right at Mr. Warren's side and asked what Molly thought were a lot of boring questions.

At least Mr. Warren didn't seem to be drinking whiskey anymore. He looked kind of pale and trembly by the time they got back to the house, but Molly was pretty sure that was just because he was tired and his leg was hurting—they'd gone the long way around, up through some neighboring woods and then back along the road. Feeling anxious for him, she said as they turned into the driveway, "If I could ever help you with packing, Mr. Warren, like all your books and stuff . . . well, school gets out next week, so after that I'll have a whole lot of extra time."

Mr. Warren had been telling Sean about going on partridge hunts here in these same woods back when they were all owned by one person, some millionaire who'd died or moved away. Now he rested a hand on one of the stone gateposts and turned his head inquiringly toward Molly. "What was that, Molly?"

Molly repeated her offer, adding that Sean would help too, and Sean nodded solemnly—though Molly knew from the packing they'd already done at home that his idea of filling a carton was to put a few things in the bottom and then pile a lot of newspaper on top.

"Packing . . . yes, well, I'm afraid we haven't made much of a start on that yet. Awful lot of sorting to do first." Mr. Warren shook his head.

"Well, maybe we could help you with that—with the sorting."

Mom had sorted out some china and kitchen stuff and old toys that Molly had helped her put in a big carton to give to Goodwill, along with the old living-room rug, which was already rolled up and waiting for the truck to come even though they wouldn't be moving until the end of July or maybe the beginning of August. Mom said she couldn't stand the sight of it one more day, and anyway the room would be cooler without it. But that was nothing compared to all the sorting the Warrens would have to do, Molly thought worriedly, especially if they were going to go live in some really little place.

She said, "Did you get to buy that cabin you wanted? The one in Ludbury?"

Mr. Warren looked puzzled. "What cabin would that be, Molly?"

"Cottage, I mean," Molly said quickly, feeling herself flush at having used the wrong word. "Mrs. Warren told me about it—that it was nice, only kind of small, and maybe you were going to try and buy it."

"Ah, yes." Mr. Warren straightened his shoulders, letting his hand fall away from the gatepost. "Nothing settled about that yet, I'm afraid. Nice little place, though—might suit us quite well, actually. We'll see," he said, and wiped his forehead with his big handkerchief, looking up at the sky. "Muggy today—looks like we're going to get a storm before long. . . . By the way," he said to Sean as they started down the driveway, "always a good idea to carry a handkerchief when you're off on a ramble. I don't mean tissues, I mean a proper handkerchief. Never know when it'll come in handy for carrying things or tying something up or making a bandage—a tourniquet, even. . . ."

They turned onto the bricks, Mr. Warren explaining to Sean what a tourniquet was and how to make one. Molly lingered on the driveway, scratching her deerfly bites and looking at the dark rectangle of the open barn door. Maybe she should go close it if there was going to be a storm, even though the barn was empty of furniture now. She wondered what the Warrens had done with all those things, especially if they still didn't have a place to move to.

She frowned, picturing the calendar on the kitchen door at home. Mr. Warren hadn't sounded very concerned, but it was already almost the middle of June, which meant it was only a few more weeks before the Warrens were supposed to be moving out of the house. Well, maybe they had friends they could stay with, she thought uncertainly. Or they could go to a motel. Or—

Lightning flared somewhere behind her. Molly decided to

forget about the barn and hurried to join Sean and Mr. Warren, who were standing just inside the Warren's front door, still talking about woodcraft, or whatever it was called.

"Oh, Molly, speaking of books—"

Mr. Warren broke off what he was saying to limp through the archway into the living room, where he took a big leather-bound book from the top of the piano. "My wife set this aside for you. Can't imagine why she thinks you'd be interested in it, but I suppose it'll give you an idea of what the old place looked like once upon a time."

It was a photograph album, Molly saw, feeling pleased and disappointed at the same time. Only one? She'd thought the Warrens would have at least two or three. As she thanked Mr. Warren, she opened the album a crack, awkwardly, because it was heavy. The pictures had been labeled in white ink on the black paper, in a fine, spiky handwriting Molly decided must be Mrs. Warren's. "Bud and Tory harvesting the corn," she read under a cloudy snapshot of two little kids eating corn on the cob at a picnic table. Were Bud and Tory the grandchildren? She'd lost the page, but anyway, she didn't think so—the picture had looked sort of faded, and besides, from what Mr. Warren had said, the album was a really old one. Those must have been the Warrens' own children, she thought, way back when.

"Is it okay to take it home with me?" she asked; but her words were lost in a clap of thunder that made them all jump, followed by a sudden gust of wind swirling into the hallway and then the heavy patter of raindrops falling on the new summer leaves outside.

"Here it comes, all right," Mr. Warren said, flattening his hand on some mail that was about to blow off the hall table. "You two had better head for cover." He held the screen door wide so they could duck under his arm. "Too bad about the wall, eh?" he added with a chuckle. "Otherwise you could go right on through."

Clutching the album to her chest, Molly sprinted over the bricks behind Sean, almost losing her footing on a piece of wet roofing paper as she turned the corner of the house.

"Don't come in this way," Dad yelled from inside over another crack of thunder as Sean tugged at the dining room door. "Wet varnish! You'll have to go around."

By the time they rounded the house and burst in the kitchen door, Molly's hair was plastered to her face, and water was streaming from the cuffs of the long pants Mr. Warren insisted Sean wear whenever they went for a walk. They looked at each other and laughed. They were even wetter than they'd been that first day they came to the house, as wet as if they'd been in swimming.

But it didn't matter anymore, Molly thought suddenly, looking down at the sopping floor. This was their own kitchen now—and not even their whole kitchen at that, only half of it: a big friendly room that would smell of bacon and toast and maple syrup in the mornings when they came down for breakfast, with Mom at the stove in her quilted robe and Dad standing up to gulp a last cup of coffee before he left for work.

For the first time, Molly could really imagine it, the life they would have here every day, going on from this summer into fall and winter and spring and then into another summer, with school getting out again and the same smells of road tar and honeysuckle and wet grass when it rained. And it wouldn't matter—it wouldn't ever matter, not really, not even if Mom got mad at them—how much water they dripped on the kitchen floor or how silly they acted or how grubby or snowy or muddy they got, because the mailbox out on the road would have their name on it, JACKSON, in big stenciled letters, and this would be the place they came home to—this old stone house behind the rough cedar hedge, waiting patiently to take them in again.

Lightning flashed again outside the window, flinging up a tilted, bone-white image of the lawn and terrace behind a smoking silver curtain of rain. Sean stopped laughing and squelching around in his wet sneakers to look at Molly curiously. "Aren't you scared of thunder and lightning anymore?" he asked.

"Not so much, maybe. Anyway, it's only lightning I'm scared of, not thunder, dummy. But inside here . . ." Molly thought about it. "Well, this is a really old house. I guess it must have been in lots of thunderstorms. So lightning wouldn't hit it now on purpose—specially, I mean, just because I'm here."

Sean looked blank, and Molly wasn't quite sure what she meant herself, except that she felt safer, somehow, than she usually did when there was lightning around. He said importantly, "Mr. Warren says the power goes off a lot when there's a storm here—you know, like the lights go off and everything—and we should make sure to have enough candles and lanterns and stuff. And something else he said . . . oh yeah, to have extra water in bottles. Because there's a pump, see, and when the electricity goes off . . ."

Molly realized suddenly that she was still hugging the Warrens' picture album to her wet T-shirt. She grabbed some paper towels from the roll on the counter and scrubbed at the damp spots on the brown leather cover. They wouldn't all quite come out. But maybe that didn't matter too much, if the Warrens didn't ever look at it or keep it out to show people.

"Better use some of that towel on yourself, Molly," Dad said, coming into the kitchen from the back hallway. "Yuck—look at the two of you! You have a change of clothes here?" They shook their heads. "Well, I suppose it's time we knocked off anyway. You might know I'd choose a day like this to put down a coat of varnish," he said gloomily. "What's the book, Molly?"

"Oh, just something the Warrens are lending me," Molly said quickly. Although he'd never said so, she knew Dad didn't like hearing about the time she and Sean spent with the Warrens.

"Doing some clearing out, are they?" he said, going to wash his hands at the sink. "Well, it's high time. If you could see all the stuff they have on their side of the attic . . ."

Molly started to say that the album had come from the attic, so maybe the Warrens had already done some clearing out up there. Then she stopped, feeling puzzled, as if there were something she ought to have noticed just now when she was over on the Warrens' side of the house. Then she realized what it was—that there hadn't been anything to notice. The living room had looked the same as it always did, serene and gracious, with everything in its place and not a single carton in sight, not even a pile of things on a chair—with no sign, in fact, that the Warrens had started getting ready to move at all.

EIGHT

FROM THE PHOTO album, Molly learned that the Warrens had had three children—Bud (whose real name was Henry), Tory (short for Victoria), and Dick (short for Richard). It was confusing at first, because their real names were written in under their baby pictures and only gradually gave way to nicknames as they grew older. Bud and Tory had straight brown hair that got lighter in the summertime, and flashing white smiles in thin, triangular faces. They were always climbing trees or standing on their hands at the beach or clowning on the lawn in silly hats and their parents' shoes. Dick was blonder, with a round face that never seemed to get tan and a small, stubborn-looking mouth. In the pictures he mostly just stood or sat with his arms folded, looking directly at the camera. He always seemed to be wearing a clean white shirt, even in a picture that showed him on horseback out West, sitting solidly on a fat brown pony.

That was on one of their family vacations, at a ranch in Wyoming where they went for several summers. The captions said things like "Picnic at Leaning Rock" and "Trip to Crystal Springs, 1948." That one showed a line of horses with Mrs. Warren riding the one in front, turning in her saddle to smile from under a wavy-brimmed Western hat. Molly had thought Mrs. Warren might have been pretty or even beautiful when she was younger, but she hadn't been, at least not in the way Mr. Warren had been handsome, especially in his navy uniform. Hers was just a face you noticed, somehow, no matter how many other faces were in the same picture with her. Bud's face was the same way, though they didn't really look alike except maybe for the shape of their eyebrows and the way their mouths turned up at the corners just before they decided to smile.

In other vacation pictures, the family stood posed in front of ski lodges and sunlit harbors and tall gray churches in Europe—they always seemed to be taking trips. Back home, they shoveled snow after a blizzard and romped with dogs and played games of croquet on the side lawn, where the garden shed was now. As the children grew older, they stood linking arms with friends on the front steps of the boarding schools they went away to, the boys wearing jackets and ties, Tory a matching skirt and blazer. They went to parties and weddings and trimmed tall Christmas trees. The trees always stood at the end of the living room where the piano was now, Molly noticed. She made a mental note to tell her parents that was where their own Christmas tree should go.

Dick played chess with his father and caught a lot of fish in a river in Canada. He broke his arm, but later was on his school rowing team, second from the end in a line of sunstruck faces. Tory finally got her braces off. In a short white tennis dress, smiling gleefully, she held up a big silver cup. She got her hair cut short in a pixie cut and wore sweaters and pearls and started smoking cigarettes.

Meanwhile, Bud played soccer and ice hockey and baseball for his school teams, and one summer he was a camp counselor, very tan, with a whistle hanging around his neck. By the end of the album, he was in college at Princeton, raising a beer mug to the camera and wearing a strange, scruffy-looking fur coat that Molly figured out must have belonged to Mr. Warren when he was in college—"Duncan's raccoon lives to fight another day," the caption said. He took a pretty, dark-haired girl in a fluffy dress to a prom. Later, on almost the last page, the same girl came to the Warrens' house. Wearing a white two-piece bathing suit, she stood poised for a dive on end of the diving board, her eyes shut tight in concentration, while Bud sat on the edge of the pool looking up at her.

It was a little like reading a story, Molly thought, one that broke off suddenly in the middle. The house made a story too, the way it changed and grew in the pictures, but at least she knew how that story came out. Once there had been more outbuildings behind the barn, including a chicken house—there was a picture of Tory gathering eggs when she was around Molly's age—and a grape arbor that had been taken down when they added the pool. Cows had grazed in the next-door field, which stretched a long way up the road, past where Jason's house was now. And of course all the trees and bushes had grown higher and shaggier since then, except for some that had vanished, like a tall shade tree that had once stood where the driveway met the road.

But the house itself didn't look too different now from

the way it did at the end of the album. At least you could still recognize it, Molly thought, the way you probably couldn't the people—the children. It was hard to realize that they'd be middle-aged now, older than her own parents.

"What happened to them?" she asked Mrs. Warren shyly when she returned the album. "I mean—where did they all go?"

"Go, Molly?" Mrs. Warren lifted her eyes from the book she was reading as she lay stretched out in a chair on the terrace. Molly had worried that she'd kept the album too long—it was Thursday afternoon before she got to go out to the house again, because Mom had been busy taking some petition around for people to sign—but Mrs. Warren had just accepted it with an absent smile and set it down on the bricks beside her chair.

"Dick and Tory and Bud . . . I was wondering what happened next." When Mrs. Warren didn't respond right away, Molly said awkwardly, in case maybe she shouldn't have used their nicknames, "Well, I guess Bud's real name was Henry—"

"Named after an uncle of Duncan's," Mrs. Warren agreed dryly, marking her place in the book with her finger. "The proverbial rich uncle, who wound up leaving everything to an African wildlife fund . . . Well, let me see. I suppose they did what children normally do, Molly—grew up and went off to college and got jobs and began living lives of their own."

Molly hesitated, knowing she was probably being a pest and that she should let Mrs. Warren go back to reading her book. But she said, "Isn't there another one? Another picture album I could look at?"

After a pause, Mrs. Warren said, "No, I don't think so, dear. Just odd snapshots. . . . Anyway, it was this period I thought would interest you, when the children were all growing up here at the house." She smiled a little, gazing over the lawn. All the workmen had left for the day and Mom was upstairs getting ready to start painting in Sean's bathroom, so it was very quiet, the sun still high and golden in the sky because they were getting close to the longest day of the year. "We did have some good times, didn't we?"

Molly nodded. "I think you had a neat life," she said.

"A neat life." Mrs. Warren laughed, and had to put a hand over her book to keep it from sliding off her lap. More quietly, she said, "Yes, Molly, I suppose we did."

She closed her eyes, still smiling, and Molly thought how she'd hardly ever seen Mrs. Warren lying back in a chair in this relaxed, tired-seeming way. Usually when she sat on the terrace she chose one of the upright chairs and worked on her needlepoint. She was wearing a white sleeveless blouse and a faded green denim skirt, and her smile made deep crevices and creases out of lines that had still been faint in the pictures, no more than light pencil strokes on the surface of her face.

Thinking again of the pictures, Molly said, "That girl-friend of Bud's . . . I wondered if they ever got married, maybe."

"Oh, my dear, Bud and his girlfriends!" Mrs. Warren stirred and crossed her ankles, looking amused. "After a while, we simply lost track."

"Her name was Paula," Molly persisted. "She looked nice. Really pretty, and—I don't know—special."

"Paula?" Mrs. Warren lay very still. "I hadn't realized

there was a picture of Paula in that old album. But yes, of course—Bud took her out a few times when they were still in college. Then they each got involved with someone else and lost touch, and it was several years before they ran into each other again. At a party, was it? Yes, in San Francisco. Bud had just finished up his stint in the air force."

Molly sat down gingerly on the edge of a light plastic chair, hoping Mrs. Warren was getting into one of her remembering moods and would go on. But she didn't; she let her voice trail away and then cleared her throat. "Yes," she said. "Paula was special. And yes, Molly, she and Bud did marry. What a perceptive child you are, to be sure."

She turned her head and twinkled her eyes at Molly, but her voice sounded strained, as if something had gone wrong with Bud and Paula, Molly thought—as if maybe they got divorced or weren't happy together or something.

She knew she was asking too many questions, but she said, "Did they have any children?"

"Yes. Two children—Ruth and Peter." Mrs. Warren looked down, smoothing the cover of the book with one hand. "Ruth was born when Bud was still at Harvard Law, and Peter a few years later."

Molly waited for her to say something more. When she didn't, she asked, "Are they the ones that live so far away?" Because they must be the grandchildren whose pictures were in the silver frame on Mrs. Warren's dresser, she decided. Mr. Warren hadn't mentioned having any others, and besides, the names sounded right, somehow.

Mrs. Warren had her eyes closed again, and for a moment Molly thought she hadn't heard. Then she nodded. Molly was starting to ask just where it was they lived and how old they were now when Mrs. Warren shifted in her chair, gave Molly a brisk little smile, and said, "Well, now, where were we? Oh yes, I was telling you about the children leaving home. . . . Well, let me see. Tory went to Radcliffe and majored in art history, and then got a job in Paris. She's been there ever since, more or less. Dick went to Harvard and then on to business school at Stanford and made a lot of money in real estate in Texas, of all places. He has a large and perfectly hideous modern house in Houston and grows roses as a hobby, the big, bright kind that have no fragrance whatever. I believe he wins prizes for them."

Molly smiled—that sounded like Dick somehow. But she also felt relieved to know that Dick was rich. So Dad had been right, she thought; the Warrens did have something to fall back on. He could take care of them if they ever needed it, like Dad had taken care of Grammy and Grandpa John. She thought of what Mrs. Warren had said about Tory and asked quickly, in case she was getting ready to read her book again, "Didn't Tory ever get married?"

"Oh, indeed. Tory's been well married—three times, to be precise. Which also means she's gone through three alimonies. Tory always did have expensive tastes. Now she lives on her friends, I believe." Mrs. Warren glanced at Molly and said, "Oh, I don't mean she takes money from them, dear, just that she does a lot of visiting here and there. The people she knows are very chic, the kind who move around a great deal, following the seasons and whatever places happen to be in fashion at the moment."

"Like the jet set, you mean?"

"Yes, I suppose so. Café society, we used to call it. . . . At any rate, Tory moves with them. I'm sure she's a delightful guest, witty and decorative and up on all the latest books and plays and so on. And of course she does know her paintings—I believe she advises a number of her friends on their collections. . . . I imagine she's also a useful fourth at tennis or golf or whatever the current sport requires. Tory's a good athlete and still keeps herself in shape." Mrs. Warren was silent for a moment. "Yes, even when she was a little girl, Tory was always in great demand as a guest. The mothers of her friends were always asking to 'borrow' her."

Remembering the lively, vivid face in the pictures, Molly could see how that would be true. But she couldn't help feeling a little sorry for Tory. Being a guest didn't seem like much of a life, no matter how nice people were to you. And Mrs. Warren's tone was so distant, as if Tory were no more to her either than someone else's guest, instead of the daughter she'd picked blueberries with and tied party sashes for and taught to ice-skate on clumsy-looking double-bladed skates down on the frozen pond.

She said, "Don't you ever see her anymore?"

"Oh, once or twice a year Tory and her friends come to New York for a week or so," Mrs. Warren said with a shrug. "And then, if it's convenient . . ." She didn't finish her sentence; instead she said slowly, "Sometimes I think if Tory had had children, things might have been different. I know she wanted them at one time, but—" She shook her head. "And now, of course, it's too late."

"What about Dick?" Molly asked. "Didn't he have children either?"

"No. Dick never married. Too selfish." Again Mrs. Warren glanced at Molly's face; this time she gave a little snort of laughter. "I expect you think that's a dreadful way for a parent to speak of a child, Molly. But it's true. Dick was born selfish . . . or cold; perhaps that's a better word. We tried spoiling him, we tried ignoring him, but nothing made any difference. Dick simply wasn't interested in other people—in receiving love or affection, let alone in giving it. Some people just are that way, you know. As if something were . . . left out."

She laced her fingers together on her lap, staring out over the sun-dappled lawn once more.

"But Bud," Molly said, feeling a kind of urgency. "Bud wasn't like that, was he?"

"Molly!"

Mom was calling her. She twisted around in her chair to see her mother standing at the far end of the terrace, beyond the rock pile, her hands on her hips. She looked mad about something. "Molly, will you come here for a minute, please?"

"I better go," Molly said hastily to Mrs. Warren, who only nodded without turning her head.

"I thought I asked you to finish unloading the car," Mom said when Molly had clambered over the rocks. "I need the vacuum cleaner upstairs right now, not an hour from now." Mom's back had been hurting from all the bending and lifting she'd been doing, and now she was trying not to move anything heavy.

"I'm sorry," Molly said, following her around to the car. "I forgot." As she leaned into the backseat, struggling to get a grip on the handle of the vacuum cleaner among all the coils of hose, Mom said, "What were you and Mrs. Warren having such a long conversation about, anyway?"

"Oh . . . things. You know, like about the olden days."

"Olden days." Mom gave a dry little laugh that sounded almost like Mrs. Warren's. "Well, I'm glad she has time to sit around thinking about them. Me, I'm just trying to survive the nowadays."

She stood watching Molly back awkwardly out of the car and then said in a softer tone, "You miss Grammy a lot, I guess, don't you, hon?"

Molly nodded, not getting the connection.

"It's a shame your other grandmother lives so far away. I realize you hardly know her, but I think the two of you would get along really well. I'm hoping she and Dad can come for a nice, long visit after we get settled in here. Not like last time, when they had to stay in a motel, remember? Now we'll have a regular guest room for them, and they can have their own TV up there and everything. . . ."

She followed Molly into the house, watching to make sure she didn't bump the vacuum cleaner against any of the freshly painted door frames and talking about how maybe her mother—Grandmother Prentiss, who lived in Hawaii and who Molly remembered dimly as a quiet, sweet-faced lady who always set the table with the best table mats— might teach Molly things like how to knit and how to make her special lemon chiffon cake. It was only after Molly had hauled her burden up the back stairs and set it down at last in Sean's room that she understood what Mom was really talking about—she thought the reason Molly liked being with Mrs. Warren was that she was lonely for a grandmother.

The idea made Molly angry and indignant in a way she couldn't quite explain. It made her seem babyish, for one thing; for another, it made Mrs. Warren not seem to count for anything in herself, as if her age was the only important

thing about her. But it wasn't like that, Molly thought. She
was friends with Mrs. Warren in a way that had nothing
to do with age or with wanting to be related. In fact, she
couldn't imagine ever feeling just ordinary and comfortable
and easy with Mrs. Warren like you would with a grandmother. But that was okay, because it was all part of what
she liked about Mrs. Warren—her being so different and
separate and not at all like anyone she'd ever known.

"Oh, I can hardly wait until we can use those nice, wide
front stairs instead of having to lug everything up the back
way," Mom was saying, looking around for an outlet near
the bathroom to plug the vacuum cleaner into. "Hand me
the brush attachment, will you, hon, there's all this sawdust
to get up. . . . Two more weeks until we have the place to
ourselves. I can hardly wait!" she said again; and added
quickly, misunderstanding the expression on Molly's face,
"I know you'll miss the Warrens, sweetie, but maybe you
can go visit them sometime in their new place. I gather
they're planning to stay in this area."

Molly opened her mouth and shut it again. She couldn't
have made herself heard anyway over the whine of the
vacuum cleaner. Besides, maybe she was wrong. Maybe the
Warrens did have a place to go to; maybe the reason there
still weren't any cartons in the living room, at least as much
of it as she'd been able to see through the glass doors, was
that they were starting their packing upstairs.

She wandered over to the window seat, now painted a
bright blue to match one of the main colors in the plaid
wallpaper. Down on the terrace, Mrs. Warren was sitting
just as Molly had left her, looking out across the lawn, the
book lying closed on her lap.

 NINE

"I JUST DON'T see how we can," Dad was saying, leaning his elbows on the mantel and running his hands through his hair. "Look, I realize they've got a problem, but so do we. I guess we could wait on taking down the other walls, but there's no way we can reschedule the work on the kitchen. It's going to be tight as it is, getting everything done before we move in."

"But if they're willing to put up with the inconvenience . . ." Mom began.

"Inconvenience! It's going to be a mess—plaster and sawdust all over the place. With all the old cabinets coming out, and then the new plumbing that has to be done, and the rewiring, there just isn't going to *be* any kitchen for a while. Oh, I suppose they could do their cooking on a hot plate or something, but what about refrigeration? What about a water supply?"

"The water won't be turned off that much of the time," Mom pointed out. "And they could always use the powder room for washing dishes. As for a fridge, they could probably move that little one of theirs into the living room easily enough."

It was Monday night, the beginning of the last week in June, and the Warrens had called to ask for an extension of their lease. They wanted to be allowed to stay on in the house for an extra two weeks, until the middle of July.

This was just what Molly had been worried might happen. She said anxiously, "What if they still can't find a place to move to? After the two weeks are over, I mean?"

Her parents looked at her distractedly. Mom said, "That's not the problem, Molly—they have a place, some house they've bought over in Ludbury. The problem is it won't be ready in time. They've just found out it needs a whole new septic system, and the earliest they can get a contractor to start work on it is the middle of next week. And since I guess it means digging up most of the front yard—"

"You'd think the Warrens would have been ready for a nice modern apartment by now," Dad interrupted sourly. "But no, they have to go on doing the country-living bit. 'A pleasant little cottage'—I can just see it. All very charming and picturesque, and probably ready to fall down around their ears."

Mom sighed and sat down on the end of Dad's recliner chair. After a moment she slid back and stretched out gingerly, as if her back was hurting again. She said, "Well, we can't just kick them out." When Dad was silent, scowling down into the empty fireplace, she added, "Barry, you know we can't. Listen, I'm not happy about it either. I've been counting the days until the walls come down and we can get to work on their side of the house. Do you know I can't even remember what color the carpet is in the upstairs hall?"

She sighed again. "Well, at least it'll mean two more weeks' rent money."

"You better believe it," Dad said grimly. "And at the same rate too, kitchen or no kitchen. As far as I'm concerned, we're doing them a favor. If they have the nerve to ask for a reduction—"

"Oh, I'm sure they won't," Mom said, and glanced at Molly, who was sitting against the wall on the rolled-up rug that Goodwill still hadn't come to pick up. "Molly, call Sean in, will you? It's almost his bedtime."

Molly twisted around to look out the open window above her head. It was still light outside, a warm, hazy evening with swallows darting around against a lavender sky. "He's just over across the street, at the Meyers'." Kenny Meyer was washing his new car again that he'd gotten for high-school graduation, hosing suds off the windshield while Sean stood at a respectful distance. Sometimes Kenny let him polish the hubcaps when he was all done.

"Well, I still want him in. No, don't just yell out the window, Molly—go out on the porch and call him."

Molly obeyed, but kept close to the screen door so she could still hear what her parents were saying. She felt relieved that the Warrens had been able to buy the cottage they wanted, after all—at least it sounded like the same one. She wondered if the new septic system was going to cost them as much as it had cost her parents to fix the leak in the roof.

"I guess I'd better tell them about the driveway too, while I'm at it," Dad was saying inside. "They'll just have to park their car up on the road for as long as it takes." Mom said something, and he said, "Two or three days, probably, and no, I don't know when—I made a deal with Tom Faye to take a few loads of blacktop off him when he does the town roads over that way. Anyhow, once the stuff's down, I don't want so much as a cat walking across it until it's good and dry."

Sean was coming up the front walk, looking sulky. "It isn't time yet," he said.

"Yes it is," Molly told him. She nodded her head at the door behind her and whispered, "The Warrens are going to stay longer. Mom and Dad don't want them to, but they are."

Sean only shrugged. He really was in a bad mood, Molly thought. "I just wish we'd move if we're going to," he muttered, kicking at the bottom step with his bare foot. "It's not like we really even live here anymore, in this crummy old house."

"It's not a crummy old house," Molly said automatically; but she knew what he meant about moving. Mom and Dad had already started taking things over to the Warrens' house, a few at a time—not just stuff they weren't using, like winter blankets and extra lamp shades, but things they were used to seeing around that Mom said were easier to take in the car than to pack, like the china ornaments from the living-room mantel and the big gold fireplace fan and the blue-and-white plate with the windmill on it that had always hung next to the kitchen door. Every day the house looked a little barer and less familiar—and smaller too, Molly thought, almost as if it were shrinking around them; as if all of a sudden they really had outgrown it.

Sean was hauling himself up along the porch railing, wriggling along it on his stomach. He wasn't wearing a shirt, only shorts. Molly looked with distaste at the fresh mosquito bites on his shinny brown back and said, "You'll get a splinter. Anyway, you better go in or Mom'll be mad."

"They're talking," he said.

"No, Dad's calling the Warrens back."

But maybe he'd finished, because now they heard him say, "Remind me to call Seldridge's tomorrow about renting a tree saw. We need to get those apple trees down before we do the driveway."

Molly and Sean exchanged glances. Sean scrambled down from the railing and followed Molly inside.

"Oh, *please* don't let that door bang every single time you come in and out," Mom said from the recliner chair, where she was still stretched out.

"What did Dad mean about the apple trees?" Sean demanded.

"We can't cut them down!" Molly said. "I don't even care about soccer; I can play on the driveway or—"

"Kids, for heaven's sake!" Mom rubbed her forehead with the back of her hand. "We're only talking about two of the trees, and it's nothing to do with soccer, Molly; it's to make room for a turnaround down by the garage."

"One of the trees is shot anyway," Dad said, coming in from the kitchen with a sandwich in his hand. "Trunk's spilt right down to the ground, and it's all rotted inside."

"But that's the special tree!" Sean said. He explained about its having been hit by lighting, and also some other stuff Molly hadn't known, about the apples being a really old variety you couldn't even buy anymore. She tried not to look at Dad's sandwich. Mom hadn't felt much like cooking tonight, and they'd had only cold cuts and potato salad for supper. Molly was pretty sure potato salad had a lot of calories in it, so all she'd had to eat were a few slices of ham and a pickle.

Dad sighed. "Look, Sean, that tree's going to go sooner or later anyway. And the apples wouldn't be any good for eating, not from trees that old that have probably never even been sprayed. Besides, even with two gone, we'll still have—what, six or seven trees left in the orchard."

"I don't see why we have to cut *any* down," Sean said, scowling.

"It's so we can have some extra space for cars to turn around in," Mom explained again, in her superpatient voice, the one she used when she really felt like yelling at them. "Like if we have guests or a party, so they don't have to back all the way up the driveway, especially in winter. Also, we thought it would be fun for you and Molly—more room for riding your bikes."

Unwillingly, Molly pictured it—the smooth blacktop paving widening out at the bottom, how you'd be able to make a big swoop on your bike all the way from the top of the driveway to around back of the garage, where the basketball net was going to be. It would be even better fun with a skateboard, if Dad would ever let them have one. From Sean's expression, she could tell that he was seeing the same picture.

She said, "Well, couldn't we wait till the Warrens leave, at least? To cut the trees down?" Sean nodded vigorously.

"No," Dad said, He was beginning to sound mad. "Come on, Molly, all the paving's got to be done at the same time, you can see that. I'm sorry if taking down a decrepit old apple tree is going to hurt Mr. Warren's feelings, but—"

He looked at them both and gave an exasperated laugh. "Nothing like having the kids on your side, eh?" he said to Mom. To Molly and Sean he said, "Those trees are coming down just as soon as I can make the necessary arrangements, and I don't want to hear another word about it. Understood?"

There was a silence. Molly and Sean didn't look at each other. Mom pushed herself carefully to a sitting position, the recliner locking itself back into place, and said, "All right, Sean, upstairs. You don't have to take a bath tonight, I guess, but wash your feet before you get into bed. And Molly, please take the full laundry basket up with you when you go—it's on top of the dryer. You can just leave it in the hall."

Sean went silently toward the stairs. Molly started to follow, but in the doorway she turned and said, "Mrs. Warren says you wouldn't be having trouble with your back if you got regular exercise and lost some weight. She says it's usually people with weak stomach muscles that get bad backs. And also . . ."

She looked down, knowing she'd already said enough but deciding to go ahead anyway. "Also I think you should leave the rhododendron bushes the way they are. They look nice from inside, and they'll be pretty in the winter too, with snow on them." She was thinking of one of the pictures in the Warrens' album, but she didn't try to explain that.

Dad was frowning at her, but Mom just took a deep breath and let it out again slowly. She said, "Thank you, Molly. That's very helpful, I'm sure. When I finally get myself moved into Mrs. Warren's house and am not feeling bone tired every minute of the day, I'll be sure to find time for regular exercise. As for the rhododendrons—we aren't planning to rip them out, you know, just cut them off some at the top. I think even Mrs. Warren would agree they've gotten pretty overgrown."

Molly hesitated, not knowing what to make of her mother's tone; also, she'd spent enough time watching Mrs. Warren gardening to be pretty sure you shouldn't just shave off the tops of special plants as if you were trimming a hedge. Finally she said, "I think there's probably a special way to cut them, if you still want them to look good and have flowers and everything. I could ask Mrs. Warren, if you want."

"Yes, Molly," Mom said. "You do that."

That week the pool got filled in. It took a long time, but finally bright blue water danced and shimmered all the way up to the mermaids and dolphins of the special tiles around the edge, and the pool was no longer just a big box sunk in the ground but a magic place. Molly got to invite Liza out for the day on Friday to try it out. Liza hadn't been to the house before, so before they went swimming she walked around looking at everything critically.

"It's nice," she said finally as they stood in the dining room, surveying the shiny wood floor and the red-and-gold-striped wallpaper.

Molly thought the wallpaper made the room sort of dark, even with the new brass candlesticks on the mantel that Mom said "picked up" the gold stripe and the crinkle-foil fan from Hubbard Street she'd put in the empty hearth below. When she had time, she was going to shop for candles the exact same shade of red as the wallpaper—crimson, she called it.

"What's supposed to go there?" Liza asked, pointing at the chain hanging from the ceiling.

"One of those big lamps with all the little things hanging down. A chandelier," Molly said, remembering the word. "Mom's been looking for an old one—you know, an antique—but they cost a whole lot, so we might have to get a new one instead. They make them *look* old, though."

Liza nodded. "Yeah. You don't want to have everything too new-looking in a house like this." For a moment her gaze lingered on the glossy new fruitwood table and eight matching chairs that had been delivered just yesterday. They were getting a matching breakfront too, with etched-glass doors, only it hadn't come yet.

Molly had been looking forward to introducing Liza to Mrs. Warren, to show her not all her friends were just silly and babyish like Amy, but the Warrens weren't home. Probably they'd gone to Ludbury, Molly thought. She still hadn't found out much about the cottage beyond the fact that it was on a nice, quiet country road and had a little brook running through the back part of the property.

"I do love the sound of running water," Mrs. Warren had said, pausing with a handful of silverware that she was transferring from a kitchen drawer to a card table in the living room—they were having to empty out their whole kitchen before the false wall came down. Her eyes had a bright, dreamy light in them as she went on, "And there's a perfect spot for a rock garden, something I've never had here. . . ." But when Molly had asked how many rooms the cottage had, she had just said vaguely, "Oh, it's small, dear. But we'll manage, I'm sure."

Again, there was no sign of the Warrens on Saturday until late afternoon, when Molly saw the old Volvo turn in between the gateposts and park beside the bricks, as if maybe they were going out again later. Sure enough, at around six, when Mom and Dad were getting ready to leave, closing and locking all the windows—they were careful about that now there was stuff in their side of the house— Mrs. Warren leaned out her front door to ask Molly if she would help her look for an earring she'd dropped in the hall.

"I think it rolled under that little chest—yes, over on the right there. . . . Thank you, dear," she said as Molly handed her the gleaming single pearl with its delicate gold clip. She was wearing a rustly black dress with a square neckline and a strand of pearls that matched the earrings. "Duncan, are you almost ready?" she called over her shoulder, standing at the mirror while she adjusted the earring and tucked a wave of hair into place.

"You look very nice," Molly said, and added, in case it sounded like Mrs. Warren didn't always look nice, "I really like all your clothes."

"Do you, Molly?" Mrs. Warren smiled at her from the mirror. "So do I, to tell the truth, although Lord knows I ought to be tired of them by now, I've had most of them so long. Still, I always did try to buy good quality, and I stopped worrying long ago about being fashionable. . . . Actually, I find most things come back into fashion if you just wait long enough," she added with a laugh. "I think this is the third time around for this particular dress."

Mom was just the opposite about clothes, Molly thought. She hated spending a lot of money on any one thing, and if a saleswoman said something like "Well, of course this is a classic, you can wear it forever" Mom would make a face and say "Who wants to wear anything forever?" and go look at something else. Molly had been clothes shopping with her just a few days ago, when they were in a big department store and Mom decided she couldn't look at one more fabric sample. She said why didn't they go up to the third floor instead, where the clothes were, so they did, but she didn't end up buying anything. Molly knew why, from the way Mom tugged at zippers and waistbands and kept turning sideways and trying to flatten her stomach with her hand. That night at supper she had only one helping of spaghetti, just like Molly. She hadn't used the word *diet* yet, any more than Molly had, but Molly was pretty sure they were both on one now.

As if Mrs. Warren had read her thoughts, she said, "You really have lost some weight, haven't you, Molly? I saw you out at the pool in that snappy new bathing suit—at least I suppose it's new." Molly nodded, smiling a little at the word *snappy*, and pushed back the bangs that always fell into her eyes when her hair started to need cutting again. Mrs. Warren noticed the gesture and said, "Have you ever thought of wearing your hair straight back, Molly? Here—like this."

She drew Molly over to the mirror and scooped Molly's fine, slippery brown hair back from her forehead. Her hand felt dry and cool. "See? You have a nice, even hairline here in front. If you let the bangs grow out, you could brush your hair away from your face and stop hiding those pretty blue eyes of yours."

Molly looked at her reflection, feeling half-pleased and half-embarrassed. She did look better, but . . . "I don't think it would stay," she said.

"Not without a band," Mrs. Warren agreed. "I don't

mean one of those rolled-up rags I see some girls wearing across their foreheads, but a proper headband. You could have them in different colors, to go with your clothes."

Molly knew the kind she meant, but no one she knew wore their hair that way, only little kids sometimes. Except . . . She frowned, trying to remember where she'd seen a girl her age wearing a blue hair band that matched her eyes. She'd had brown hair like Molly's, too.

Mr. Warren came down the stairs just then, jaunty in plaid pants and a cranberry-red jacket, and Molly realized what she'd been remembering—the picture upstairs of their granddaughter. Ruth, her name was, the daughter of Bud and Paula.

"Time we were on our way, dear," Mr. Warren said to his wife, as if it had been she who'd kept him waiting. "Elaine Chapman always did like her guests to be prompt."

Mrs. Warren gave a snort, tucking a beaded evening purse under her arm. "Yes, and she was a good half-hour late the last time she came here."

"Well, but that was when Murray was so ill, remember? Some problem with one of the nurses she'd hired . . . it was just before he had to go back into the hospital."

For a moment, a shadow crossed their faces. Then Mrs. Warren said briskly, "Well, at least we won't have to stand around admiring Murray's dahlias this year. Dreadful, stiff plants, and such horrid colors—like a row of giant lollipops."

"Unless Elaine decided to plant them again. You know, a living memorial kind of thing."

They both chuckled, and for a moment Molly felt shocked, realizing they were talking about someone who had died. Then she thought that when you were the Warrens' age, having your friends die must be something you got used to, in a way.

Still chuckling, the Warrens made their way carefully over the bricks to the car, Mr. Warren holding Mrs. Warren's elbow. He was shorter than she was in her high-heeled shoes—or maybe that was just because of the way his shoulders stooped over. The red jacket had a crease in the back, Molly noticed, and a thread hanging down from the center seam; she wondered if the jacket was as old as Mrs. Warren's dress. She hoped nobody at the party would notice the thread.

TEN

THE DAY AFTER the carpenters knocked down the wall between the two kitchens and began the work of prying out the old cabinets and fixtures, the work crew arrived at the house to find the door from the kitchen to the front hall locked from the other side and the swinging door blocked, too. The Warrens had nailed a board across it on the living-room side.

Dad was furious. "So the men decided it was easier to move some of the stuff out through the Warrens' side of the house instead of using the kitchen door or going around through the dining room—okay, they were wrong, and I've told them so. I can understand how the Warrens might be a bit upset. But locking us out—and not just locking, actually boarding over a door—"

"You can't lock a swinging door," Mom pointed out. "But you'd think they could have just wedged it or pushed a chair up against it or something."

"They wanted to feel 'secure,' " Dad said in the angry, mimicking voice Molly had learned to dread. "No more

workmen trampling over their precious rugs or asking to use
the phone or the bathroom, let alone breathing the same air.
Also, having the doors stay shut will help keep the plaster
dust out of their side of the house."

Mom said—trying to calm him, Molly could tell—"Well,
that's true, Barry. And there's all the noise too. I mean, you
can't blame the Warrens for feeling kind of exposed and
wanting to hang on to a little privacy. They're still paying
a good rent, after all."

"Oh, you can be sure they reminded me of that. With
which I reminded them that staying on was their idea, not
ours. They want to move out tomorrow, that's fine with
me—I'll be happy to return their check." Dad yanked at his
tie to loosen it, still fuming. "It's that board that gets me.
If they've damaged the woodwork in the living room—"

"But if it's just nail holes, couldn't you fill them in?"
Molly said, thinking of the little can of wood putty Dad
was always carrying around with him. When he glared at
her, she said, "I mean—well, aren't we going to paint the
living room anyway?"

Mom said, "She's right, you know, Barry."

Dad gritted his teeth. "Of course she's right. And of course
the Warrens can do no wrong. They really took care to
cultivate these kids of ours, didn't they? Making sure our
hands would be good and tied if things ever came to any
kind of showdown." Mom shook her head at him and started
to say something, but he held a hand up and said, letting
his breath out explosively, "Okay, okay. We'll let it go. Let
the Warrens lock themselves in if that's what they want to
do. The less I see of them in the next two weeks, the happier
I'll be anyway."

Molly was afraid he might tell her and Sean to keep away from the Warrens from now on, but he didn't. It turned out not to make much difference, though, because they were hardly ever home, and when they were, they stayed inside with the front door closed and curtains drawn across the terrace doors. From out on the lawn, Molly sometimes caught a glimpse, through the upstairs windows, of Mrs. Warren moving around in her bedroom, but when Molly waved, she never seemed to see her.

The flower beds were beginning to look really neglected now. It hadn't rained in a long time, so Molly watered them with the hose, and also pulled out some of the grass that had started growing right in with the flowers. That helped, but still, a lot of the plants seemed to be getting all tangled up with each other, and some of them looked kind of sick too, with leaves that were puckered around the edges or had big blotches on them or were getting all chewed up by bugs. Finally even Mom noticed. "What's the matter with the roses?" she said, frowning down at a bush that had some dried-up-looking buds on it and hardly any leaves. "They must need spraying or something."

"There's a lot of different spray stuff in the garden shed," Molly told her, and added, remembering the bushel baskets, "Only I guess we should ask Mrs. Warren first, if we want to use any."

"We don't have to ask Mrs. Warren anything," Mom said sharply. "Everything in that shed belongs to us now."

"It does?" Molly was surprised, remembering what Mrs. Warren had said about gardening at their new cottage. Wouldn't she want to take her spades and rakes and things with her? But of course there were quite a lot of them;

maybe she'd just saved out her favorite tools, like the red-handled trowel she always kept close to hand, the way Dad did his favorite hammer.

"Yes, and we paid quite a price for all that stuff, too," Mom told her grimly. "As much as you'd pay to get every-thing new. Of course, *they* said it was a bargain because you can't buy tools like those anymore." She shrugged. "Well, maybe they're right. . . . Anyway, Molly, I don't want you going near those cans and boxes on the back shelf. Most of that stuff is pure poison. In fact, maybe I'd better move it higher, where Sean can't get at it."

"Oh, Mom, he wouldn't," Molly said. Her parents still treated Sean like such a baby sometimes.

But Mom was already heading for the garden shed after a glance at her watch—they were waiting for a new elec-trician to come and fix some wires in the kitchen that the first electrician had done wrong. Over her shoulder, she said, "By the way, Molly, I ran into that nice Mrs. Reese again down at the Winding Ridge Market when I stopped for milk. I don't believe their prices, they're even higher than at the Village Mart in town, but it's so close, and you do meet the local people there. . . . Anyway, I didn't realize she had a daughter just your age. Kim, is that her name?"

"Kimberly," Molly said with a sigh. Mom had already forgotten about the roses, she could tell. Anyway, they wouldn't know which spray to use. If she ever got a chance, maybe she could ask Mrs. Warren.

"They live in that nice old farmhouse up the road, the one that's set way back, with the big screened-in porch," Mom went on, her voice coming out muffled from inside the shed. "She says they want to have you over as soon as we're settled in. Kim has her own pony, did you know? Mrs. Reese asked if you knew how to ride, and I said no, but I was sure you'd love to learn. . . ."

A van was pulling into the driveway on their side. Molly called that the electrician was here, and Mom backed out of the shed, careful not to get dirt on her new beige summer-weight sweater and white pants. As the door swung shut behind her, Molly caught a glimpse of something red on the wall to the left—Mrs. Warren's trowel, hanging neatly from its usual nail. Molly frowned. Mrs. Warren must just have forgotten it was still there, she decided. That would be another thing to mention, next time she saw her.

The morning the driveway was scheduled to be paved over, Dad drove out to the house early, taking Molly with him. He was using some of his vacation time now to help with all the things that still needed to be done. He'd take the rest in August, when they actually moved in.

He pulled into the space where the carport had been and got out, shading his eyes against the dazzle of morning sun-light coming through the trees behind the lower part of the barn. "Their car's still down there," he said with a frown. "Maybe they didn't see my note." He hesitated, then glanced at Molly as she slithered around the hood to join him—the metal was already burning hot from the sun, though it was still so early—trying not to crush the dusty leaves of the azalea bushes that had been amazing clouds of yellow and pink and flame-color back in the springtime. "Go make sure the Warrens know about moving their car, will you, Molly? And tell them they'd better do it right away—the crew could be along any time now."

The green Volvo had been in the garage for several days now, all the time the apple trees were coming down and the kennel fencing was being torn out and trucks were driving in and out with fill for the lower part of the driveway. The whining, droning snarl of the tree saw had seemed to go on for a long time. Dad had the high-school boys cut the wood up for firewood, saying there was nothing like having apple logs to burn on a winter night. Molly and Sean had kept looking up at the library door, expecting Mr. Warren to appear, but he never did. Even yesterday, when a road scraper had come in to smooth over the worst of the old ruts, raising a great cloud of dust and making a clatter that seemed to rattle all the windows on both sides of the house, there had been no sign of the Warrens.

"Go on," Dad said now, giving Molly a little push. "They won't bite you," he added with a wry grin. "Me, maybe, but not you."

Molly still hadn't seen the Warrens to talk to since the night they went to the dinner party, and she knew Dad never talked to them at all anymore if he could help it. That was why he'd slid the note about the driveway under their front door instead of calling them. So she couldn't help feeling a little funny about breaking in on them now, even if it was for a good reason.

She hesitated, then headed down toward the terrace, going the long way around past the rock pile that by now seemed almost a natural part of the landscape, with weeds and grass growing through the crevices. Dad still planned to build the barbecue himself, though Mom said they should hire a mason unless he was looking forward to brushing off the snow as he worked. Molly knew it would probably be politer to use the front door, but the terrace doors seemed friendlier somehow, even all curtained over like they were with the faded rose-colored drapes.

"Yes, Molly?"

It was Mr. Warren who answered her knock, after what seemed like a long time. He was still in his bathrobe and didn't look as if he'd shaved yet. In fact, he didn't look too good at all, Molly thought in dismay. There were pouches under his eyes, and his shoulders seemed even more stooped than she remembered them, making his chest look sort of hollow and caved in. Also, the hand that held the door was shaking—not a lot, but enough so she couldn't help noticing.

She delivered her message, trying to see past Mr. Warren into the living room. It smelled of food—coffee and something else that wasn't so nice, more like garbage; she'd forgotten about the Warrens' having to do all their cooking in there. She could see the boarded-over kitchen door with the refrigerator crammed into the corner next to it, and in front of that the table where she and Sean had sat to have their hot chocolate, set now with breakfast things and a squat, old-fashioned toaster.

"Oh, indeed, we got the note," Mr. Warren told her. "But the car will be all right where it is. We don't plan on going out in the next day or so. Thank your father for taking the trouble to check, though, Molly."

"Well, but it might be longer than that," Molly said quickly as Mr. Warren started to close the door again. "Dad said maybe three days, to make sure the driveway is really dry."

"In this weather? Oh no, I think two ought to do it. Today's going to be a scorcher." He blinked into the sunlight, looking out across the dew-silvered lawn. "See that little haze there, to the south, and the way you can see the backs of the birch leaves? That almost always means a fine, hot day."

Mr. Warren's voice sounded stronger now, with the note of relish it always had when he talked about weather and outdoor things. Feeling encouraged, hoping he wouldn't shut the door again right away, Molly said, "Is your new cottage ready yet? I mean, did they get the hole all filled back up again and everything?"

"The hole," Mr. Warren said, in that way he had of repeating what you said to him. "Ah no, not yet, Molly. Makes things difficult, you know, getting in and out."

"I guess you have to use planks," Molly said, nodding, remembering a building site she used to pass on her way to school.

Mr. Warren gave a sudden laugh that turned into one of his coughing fits. Molly waited anxiously while he caught his breath, but when he straightened up he looked better than he had before, some of the color back in his cheeks. "Yes, I guess you could say that's what we're doing these days, Molly—walking the plank." He chuckled some more, then tilted his head back and sniffed the air. "A beautiful summer morning, to be sure."

He stood still in the doorway for a moment, and Molly thought maybe he was looking down at the place where the special apple tree had been; but all he said was, "Summer —the most beautiful word in the language, I've always thought," and turned back into the living room. Now he seemed to notice the same smell Molly had, because he said, "There is one thing you might do, Molly, if it's not too much trouble, and that's to take this bag of trash up to the road. Garbage truck will be along later, and if it can't come down the driveway . . ."

He bent down, fumbling with the tie of a plastic garbage bag, and now Molly could see all the way into the beautiful room. It was crowded and untidy and piled so high with cartons at the far end that you couldn't even see the piano anymore. The sight made her feel sad but also relieved, as if she could finally let out a breath she'd been holding inside herself for a long time. It looked like the Warrens would be ready to move in time after all.

"Not too heavy for you, is it?" Mr. Warren asked, handing her the bag. Molly shook her head; actually it felt surprisingly light to be someone's garbage for a whole week, if that was as often as the truck came. "Well, now, I'd better get a fresh pot of coffee going on this gadget of ours"—the hot plate, he meant, which Molly could see on top of the refrigerator—"or my wife will have my head."

Molly said, looking at the cartons, "I could help do some other things too, if you want. I'm pretty strong."

"That's very kind of you, Molly. But we manage all right—just do a bit at a time, you know. Besides, I'm sure your parents have plenty of jobs to keep you busy with, over on the other side."

His tone was pleasant and he gave her a smile as he closed the door, but there was a chill in his blue eyes that made Molly realize unhappily how little liking there was now between the Warrens and her parents.

If only things weren't that way, she thought, walking slowly up to the road with the garbage bag, there was probably a whole lot of stuff she and Sean could do to help the

Warrens with their move. Maybe, too, they wouldn't be keeping themselves all shut in like they'd been doing. She didn't think it could be healthy for them, staying indoors all the time. For just a moment, looking at Mr. Warren in his cotton bathrobe and worn leather slippers, Molly had had a troubling memory of Grandpa John at the nursing home in Florida the one time she'd been taken to see him. Hardly any of the old men there had on daytime clothes, not even the ones that were up and around instead of being in a wheelchair like Grandpa John. Too much trouble to keep changing back and forth, he'd said with a shrug, and besides, who was around to care?

Molly shook the thought away; she was just being dumb—it was early in the morning still, not even eight o'clock yet, so why shouldn't Mr. Warren be in his bath-robe? She set the garbage bag down on the grass verge of the road beside the Warrens' mailbox and walked along to the other driveway. She was just turning down it when a voice on her right said "Psst!" in a loud whisper.

She knew without looking who it would be—Jason, sure enough, crouched in the long grass of the field, beckoning to her from behind a tall clump of black-eyed Susans.

Molly hated being said "Psst!" to. "What?" she said coldly, coming to a halt in the middle of the cement strip, which had oil spots on it now from all the trucks and vans that had parked there.

"I saw you talking to old Warren just now," Jason said, sidling forward a few feet. His eyes were gleaming in the way that always filled Molly with distaste. "I bet he was real hung over, right?" Molly stared at him. "That's what he does at night," Jason went on, pointing at the terrace.

"Sits out there and drinks. And *she* goes out and walks around in this real slow, spooky way, like she was a ghost or something. Maybe she's going to come back and haunt you," he added with a giggle.

Molly took a step toward the fence. "You're a liar and a creep, Jason Chandler," she said in a fierce, low voice. "If my parents ever find out you've been hanging around here at night—"

"But that's why I'm telling you," Jason said. His voice was whiny, but for once he held his ground. "Like, the Warrens are getting really weird now, and maybe your parents should know about it—about how they act when they think no one's around to see them. I wouldn't tell Sean," he added virtuously.

"Go away," Molly said with loathing. "Just go away, will you, Jason?"

"I haven't even told you the main thing," Jason said, hunching his shoulders and dropping his voice so that Molly had to take a few more unwilling steps toward the fence. "Sometimes they go over in your side of the house at night. They take flashlights, and you can see them moving around and hear them talking and laughing. Mrs. Warren was looking at some new wallpaper or something, and she said how your mom was doing her best to make a sow's ear out of a silk purse, and they both laughed. I don't know what that means, but it didn't sound too nice, the way she said it."

Molly hadn't realized the Warrens still had keys to the empty side of the house. Then she thought that of course they wouldn't need them; they could just unlock the hall door into the kitchen and go on through, now that the wall was down in there. As she thought this, she also thought of the empty bottle she'd felt inside the garbage bag, bumping against her leg as she walked; and even though she told herself it could have been a tomato-juice or Coke bottle, not necessarily an empty whiskey bottle at all, she realized she believed Jason.

She wasn't going to let him see that, though, so she said scornfully, "You're just making it up. The Warrens wouldn't do sneaky stuff like that. They're not like you."

"Well, maybe they only did it one night," Jason said, unfazed. "But it's true, I saw them. You gonna tell your parents?" he asked avidly.

"No," Molly said, and clenched her fists. "I wouldn't tell them anything *you* said, and besides, it's none of your business. You just stay away from our property, Jason, or I'll tell your parents how you're getting out at night and sneaking around. And I'm going to tell my brother not to play with you anymore."

She must have looked as angry as she felt, because Jason backed away as if he was scared she was going to charge right through the fence at him. "Who cares about your dumb brother?" he said sulkily. "He's just a boring little kid. Besides, we're moving."

Molly was surprised out of her anger. "You are?" she said, adding quickly, "Good riddance."

"Yeah, back to California. Big deal." Jason shrugged. "This is the third time we moved in four years. My mom hates Connecticut anyway. She says it's full of snooty people like the Warrens. She says your parents will never make it with people like that—it's like a club, and they never let anyone new in."

For an instant Molly had found herself feeling almost sorry

for Jason, having to move so much—no wonder he was so creepy and didn't have any real friends. Now she looked at him in disgust and said, "My parents don't care about stuff like that anyway," and turned on her heel. Over her shoulder, she added, "I hope it's a really boiling hot day today, Jason, because you're not getting to swim in our pool anymore. I'm going to tell my mom not to invite you."

She knew her mother didn't like Jason very much anyway, and if his family was moving away, Mom wouldn't have to worry about staying in good with his mother. As for Sean, if he made a fuss Molly would just tell him what Jason had said about him being a boring little kid. Anyway, Sean was getting to be friends now with some of the kids who lived in the development on the other side of the woods; he didn't care all that much about Jason anymore.

Up on the road, there was the slow rumble of a heavy truck, followed by a whine of brakes and Dad's voice over by the main driveway, calling out directions. Molly thought she'd better tell him first chance she got about the Chandlers' house being on the market. He and Mom had talked about getting an option on the field so somebody couldn't buy it and build a house there, right smack up next to them. Molly wasn't sure what an option was, but she thought maybe they'd better see about getting one.

But she wasn't going to tell them what Jason had said about the Warrens. It was only a week more until they left anyway. She and Sean had been thinking maybe the Warrens wouldn't mind so much about leaving their house after all, now that they had the new cottage to think about and plan for. They'd decided maybe they were being dumb to even care about things like the apple trees being chopped down. The Warrens might have a whole bunch of nice old fruit trees at their new place and not even be interested anymore in what happened here.

But now she knew that they'd been wrong; and that it had been been wrong, too, to go on hoping the Warrens might get to stay on at the house a while longer, maybe even right up until the day her family moved in. It would be better for them to leave—better for them, and maybe for the house, too. The house needed breathing time, Molly thought suddenly, a time of standing empty in the summer nights and letting silence wash through it, cleansing away the old lives and making ready for the new, while overhead the constellations wheeled slowly by.

ELEVEN

"OH, BARRY, STOP worrying, will you?" It was the night before the Warrens were supposed to move, and Dad had been trying to call them to make sure everything was still on schedule and to ask them to leave their keys in the front hall; but it turned out their phone had already been disconnected. "They would have let us know if there was any problem," Mom told him.

"Yeah, I guess so." But he frowned. "Look, I know you told the Warrens we'd stay away tomorrow, and it's true I could stand to put in a day at the office, but the more I think about it—"

"No," Mom interrupted firmly. "We're leaving them alone on their last day. Imagine how you'd feel, after so many years. You wouldn't want the new owners hanging around and breathing down your neck. We may have had our differences with the Warrens, but we owe them that much consideration. Anyway," she said with a pleasurable little sigh, "it's the day after tomorrow I'm looking forward to. Imagine going out to the house and knowing they're *gone*.

It'll be the first time I'll really feel like the place belongs to us."

Molly stared at her parents. "But we *have* to go out to the house tomorrow!" she said. "I never got to say good-bye."

"Oh, Molly—"

"I have to," she insisted. "I wouldn't have gone to the fair with Amy today except you said they'd have the packers there for the lamp shades and things, and anyway I thought I could say good-bye to the Warrens tomorrow."

She could feel tears welling up in her eyes. Normally she despised people who cried to get their way, but she couldn't help it. She'd been planning how she'd knock on the War- rens' front door on their last day, when it wouldn't count as disturbing them. For one thing, she still had her gardening questions to ask Mrs. Warren—or if Mrs. Warren was too busy, maybe she could at least give Molly the name of a book that would tell about all the different flowers and how to take care of them. For another, she had a present for them, one of the cracked pool tiles that she'd mended with Elmer's Glue and made a wooden frame for.

"Tell you what, Pat," Dad said, glancing at Molly and away again. "Maybe you could swing by the house in the late afternoon tomorrow—you know, just check that every- thing looks okay—and take Molly with you."

Mom thought about it. "Well, I did want to go over to that carpet place in Holbrook some day this week—they're having a big sale on shags, forty percent off. . . . I suppose I could drop Molly off at the house for an hour or so and then pick her up on my way back."

"But what if the Warrens have already left by then?" Molly protested.

Dad shook his head at her. "That's your best deal, Molly," he told her. "Take it or leave it."

So of course she had to take it. By noon the next day Molly had her present wrapped, and after that she had to hang around the house while Mom went marketing, because Mrs. Blake was coming over to measure for some curtains. Mrs. Blake was really big now with her baby, which was supposed to get born at the beginning of September. "Let's just hope it doesn't come early," she said to Molly with a tired smile. "I don't think I could handle a new house and a new baby right at the same time."

As Molly helped put the groceries away later in the familiar wooden cupboards, so dark and cramped inside compared to the wide metal ones the men from the kitchen company were installing out at the Warrens' house, she thought how strange it was that the house on Hubbard Street could seem "new" to Mrs. Blake, the same way her baby would be new, like a blank page waiting to be written on. To Molly it felt more like an old scribbled-over school notebook that didn't have any space left in it, the kind you shoved into a desk drawer and hardly ever looked at again. Would she ever feel that way about the Warrens' house? she wondered. Right now it was hard to imagine. Somehow it felt like there would always be more space to fill up there.

"Whew, it's hot," Mom said, folding away the last paper bag. "I think I'll make a glass of iced tea and take it out on the back porch. There's lemonade in the fridge if you want some, Molly."

Molly shook her head. Frozen lemonade, she thought, and remembered Mrs. Warren's strong old fingers squeezing lemons while her rings slipped and flashed in the light. After a while, she went upstairs and changed into her new shorts and matching sleeveless top, crinkly pink cotton with narrow white and yellow stripes running through it. She brushed her hair for a long time, and even tried holding it back with the white ribbon from around the neck of the plush rabbit she'd won at the fair yesterday. But her bangs still weren't long enough, and she decided the ribbon just looked funny.

Finally Mom said it was time to go. She looked at Molly's outfit and at the flat package she was carrying so carefully, but didn't say anything. As she was backing the car out, Sean came running up with his friend Tony. When he found out where they were going, he wanted to come and bring Tony too; but Mom told him moving day would be tiring enough for the Warrens without a bunch of kids running around, that Molly was only going to stay a little while, and that anyway, he was supposed to be spending the afternoon at Tony's house.

Sean started to argue, but then shrugged and said, "Oh, well, I'd rather go see Mr. Warren when he's in his new house anyway. He says there's a little river there that might even have otters in it. You ever see an otter?" he asked Tony.

"Otters, around here?" Mom shook her head as she put the car in gear and started off along Hubbard Street. "Oh, well, if Mr. Warren says so, I suppose it's got to be true, at least as far as Sean's concerned."

Soon after they made the turn onto the blacktop road, they met the blue kitchen van coming the other way. Mom tooted her horn and pulled over, and after a moment the van stopped too. She crossed the road to speak to the driver while Molly sat in the hot car and listened to the insects zinging in the dry grass beside her. It hadn't rained in a really long time now, and Dad had started worrying about letting the Warrens cook on a hot plate in case they started a fire, even though Molly had told him they had it in a safe place, on top of their refrigerator. After today, she thought, he wouldn't have to worry about the Warrens anymore.

"Al says the moving van left about an hour ago," Mom reported, getting back into the car. "Loaded all the way up to the roof, but they got everything in, as far as he knows. He wasn't sure if the Warrens were still there or not."

They started off again. Molly sat silent with the present on her lap, watching for the bend in the road where Jason's house would come in sight, and then the field, and then the slate roof shining smooth in the sun above the tall line of the cedar hedge. "They're still here," she said, letting out her breath. "I see their car in the driveway."

Mom looked at her watch as she pulled over by the stone gateposts. The old green Volvo was parked on the glossy new asphalt opposite the library door, as if the Warrens might be inside collecting one last load. "Let's see, it's after four now—I should be back by five-thirty at the latest, depending on the traffic. Try to keep an eye on the time, will you, hon? The kitchen clock's plugged in now. I think you can see it through the window, but maybe I'd better give you the keys. You might want to go inside anyway after the Warrens leave, it's so hot out. . . . I'll pick you up around on our side, okay?"

Molly nodded, dropping the keys into the pocket of her shorts as she got out of the car. She could tell Mom didn't want to have to speak to the Warrens if she could help it —not now and not later either, if they were still around.

"I must say everything looks very neat and tidy," Mom observed. Molly had been thinking the same thing. Except for a big pile of trash down by the barn, in the regular collection place, there was hardly anything to show that today had been the Warrens' moving day. Only a trampled cigarette butt at the edge of the old bricks and some flattened-back rhododendron leaves remained to mark the path the movers must have taken all day between the driveway and the front door, carrying out load after load of cartons and rugs and lamps and furniture.

"Well, I'll see you later, hon," Mom said, glancing into the side mirror. She looked back at Molly and hesitated, frowning a little. "Are you sure you want me to leave you here, Molly? I'll be quite a while, you know. If you'd rather, I could just wait a minute while you run in and give them your present."

"No," Molly said, shaking her head, though she was tempted. She felt nervous and uneasy in a way she couldn't quite explain to herself. Actually, it was a feeling she'd been having all day, but she'd thought it would go away once she got here. Instead, it was worse.

Mom studied her for a moment and then said lightly, "Well, suit yourself. You look very nice, sweetie," she added with a smile. "Five-thirty, okay?" She drove off, her brake lights showing red at the next bend, the sharp one where Dad said they ought to have a sign put up.

Once the sound of the car had faded away, it was so quiet that Molly could hear the dry little scuff and slap her flip-flops made as she walked down the driveway and across the old bricks to the Warrens' front door. Although it must have been standing wide open earlier, the blue door was shut tight now, the way Molly had grown used to seeing it these past few weeks, heavy and solid and blank beneath its graceful fan of stone. Molly lifted the big knocker and let it bang down against the wood. The sound seemed loud, but after it died away the silence flowed back in as thickly as before. It was hot even here in the shade, with no air stirring. Molly used the knocker again, once, then twice; still there was no answer from inside the house.

She hesitated, feeling self-conscious standing there on the brick step with her present under her arm, as if she'd gone to a birthday party and found out it was the wrong day. Maybe the Warrens just didn't want to answer the door in case it was someone trying to sell them something or give them a religious pamphlet. She decided it would be okay to open it a crack and call inside, so they'd know who it was. But when she tried, she discovered that the door was locked, the iron handle stiff and unyielding under her hand.

Molly frowned. She waited a little longer, then set her package down carefully on the brick step and went around to try the library door. It too was closed and locked, in spite of the car waiting there at the end of the brick path. By standing on tiptoe, Molly could just see in through the glass panes at the top, but there was no sign of anyone moving around inside, only the empty, shadowy room with its yawning fireplace and the bare bookshelves climbing like ladders to the ceiling.

The Warrens must be outside somewhere, Molly thought, maybe around back. She squeezed her way to the rear of the house in the narrow space between the rhododendron bushes and the living-room windows, closed and locked now and stripped of their rose-colored curtains. The long room looked narrower and smaller somehow than it had when it was full of furniture, with only ghostly squares and rectan' gles on the bare floorboards to show where the glowing rugs had been. Now that it was empty she could see how badly it needed painting, too. The strip of raw wood still nailed in place across the kitchen door stood out like a gash upon the gentle, faded surface of the room.

Molly squeezed past the last bush and came out onto the terrace. All the garden furniture had gone except for the oldest and most beat'up of the plastic chairs, which still sat facing out over the lawn. There was no one in sight. Molly stood scanning the hot, bright landscape—the barn and the orchard on her left; the lawn and pool; the rosebushes and the little low hedges around the place where the birdbath used to be; the garden shed; the long flower beds, where a few brilliant spots of color still burned under the July sun. For a moment her gaze skipped nervously over the fence into the field beyond, in case Jason might be hiding there, spying on her. Then she remembered that his family was away on vacation this week at the Jersey shore.

The pool filter hummed in the silence. Molly listened for a sound of voices but couldn't hear any. She took a breath and called out the Warrens' names, but not as loudly as she might have; if they were down in the woods or over behind the barn somewhere, taking a last walk around and saying good'bye to things, maybe she shouldn't disturb them. Sooner or later, anyway, they'd be coming back up to the car. And she had plenty of time before Mom came back.

She turned toward the glass doors behind her. They glinted in the sun, giving back her own reflection, and she had to go up close in order to see in. The living room wasn't quite empty, as she'd thought. A broom and dustpan and some other cleaning things occupied the niche where the grandfather clock had been, and over on the right, under the end window, there was a row of potted plants on the floor next to a copper watering can with a long spout. The plants had been freshly watered, droplets still glistening on the leaves.

These doors at least must have been left unlocked, Molly thought, since the Warrens still had things in here to bring out. Deciding they wouldn't mind if she went inside where it was cooler for a minute, Molly twisted one of the handles. It wouldn't give, and neither would the other one. Surprised, she wiggled them both again, but it was no use. The glass doors were as securely locked as the other doors she'd tried.

She walked slowly around to the driveway, away from the hot glare of the terrace. It seemed strange that the Warrens would have locked everything up like this if they were just going for a walk. She looked at the car. Something about the car was wrong, too, she thought. Shouldn't it be full of stuff, things piled high on the backseat at least? But when she went up to it and looked inside, she saw that it was empty. The windows were open and a key chain hung from the ignition, but there wasn't anything on the worn seats or down on the floor, not even a carrier bag.

Maybe there were things in the trunk, Molly thought uncertainly; maybe they were leaving room for a whole big load of stuff that was still upstairs waiting to be brought down. But again, why lock the house?

She swiveled around to look at the upstairs windows, all tightly shut in spite of the heat. What if the Warrens were inside after all? she thought suddenly. What if something had happened to them? They might be sick, or hurt, or . . . What if one of them had fallen and the other tried to help and got hurt too? What if they'd been trying to call out for help, only she couldn't hear them with the house all closed up like it was, the stone walls muffling their cries?

Molly took a step backward and felt the chunky little weight of the keys in her shorts pocket. They were only the keys to her side of the house, she thought, but still—

Without further thought, only sure somehow that she'd been right to feel uneasy, sharp little prickles of dread min-gling now with the damp hairs at the back of her neck, Molly hurried back down to the terrace and along it to the kitchen door. It took some fumbling to find the right key and fit it in, but finally she was inside, the temporary plywood floor jouncing under her feet as she picked her way through the jumble of loose shelving and stacked For-mica and shiny new kitchen hardware to the door leading into the Warrens' front hall. She wasn't surprised to find it was still locked. But that was okay; Molly was pretty sure she knew another way into the Warrens' side of the house.

Upstairs in Sean's room, she scrambled onto the window seat, pushed open the innermost of the two windows, and dropped onto the kitchen roof. From here it was only a few yards to the other side of the false wall, where the big hall window looked out over the lawn and woods. That would have been the easy window to get in by, except that it was shut tight and worked by a little crank on the inside. Molly studied the frame for a moment but couldn't see any way of prying it open. Farther along, the first of Mrs. Warren's windows was closed, too, and set higher up; but at least it was a regular window, and Molly could tell by the little knob halfway that it wasn't locked.

Awkwardly, standing on tiptoe, she managed to shove the window open a few inches. After that it seemed to stick, but at least now she had something to grab on to. Kicking off her flip-flops, Molly backed up as far as she could to the white railing, then took a running jump at the window, hooking her fingers over the sill and scrabbling at the stone wall with her toes until she was high enough to work an elbow into the opening. With her free hand she jiggled the bottom of the window, trying to unstick it. It gave suddenly, sliding up all the way with a bang. Molly swung her legs over the sill and tumbled into the room.

It was empty, the mirror opposite her reflecting only an expanse of sea-green carpet, indented in places from the legs of furniture, and a section of wallpaper whose delicate flowers seemed to give off a faint, light perfume in the hot, still air.

"Mrs. Warren!" Molly called.

But already she could feel that she'd been wrong, that there was no one here. She went through the big old-fashioned bathroom, empty except for a sliver of soap in the dish over the basin and a frayed hand towel on one of the racks, and on into Mr. Warren's room at the front of the house. A wastebasket still stood in one corner, a tie hung limply over the knob of the closet door. But there was no big pile of things waiting to be taken down to the car, and nothing in the closet except a handful of battered wire hangers that swung lightly in the little draft she made as she opened the door.

Molly came out into the sunlit upper hall and paused to

wipe the sweat from her face with her forearm. Her heart was making a lot of noise in her chest, banging away high up under her collarbone. A movement at the big window made it stop for a moment, but it was only a bird, a hawk dropping out of the flat blue sky to hover on its fringed wings above the distant trees. There was still the rest of the downstairs to check, Molly reminded herself, the front hall and the powder room and the little room Mrs. Warren had used as an office. But she was sure now that there was nothing to find, no one lying sick or hurt anywhere inside the house. Then why did she feel so scared and trembly in the knees as she started down the stairs?

She was halfway down when she saw the note tucked onto the wide stone ledge of the window to the right of the front door, a folded sheet of paper with a bunch of keys lying on top of it. If she'd been just a little taller, she would have seen it before, when she was standing outside on the step. "Mr. Jackson" was written on the outside of the paper in Mrs. Warren's familiar spiky handwriting.

Slowly Molly opened it. She read it through once, twice; then stuffed it into the pocket of her shorts, wrestled frantically a moment with the heavy lock of the door, and left the house at a run.

TWELVE

THE GOING WAS easy down the smooth new paving of the driveway, but the grass in the orchard hadn't been cut in some time, and it dragged at Molly's ankles as she ran. Beyond the apple trees, the ground that had been all soft and spongy in the spring was lumpy now with hard little mounds of tufted grass and hollows filled with coarse green weeds. Molly stumbled several times and then had to slow down anyway, looking for the break in the stone wall that marked the way to the pond. Once Dad finished all the clearing and leveling he planned to do, there would be a broad, open track, but for now there was just the narrow path half-hidden by the trees.

She scrambled over the gap into a partial clearing, a tangle of sumac and wild berry bushes and still-green goldenrod stippled with buds. From here the path wound downhill into heavy shade, skirting a huge boulder wrinkled gray like an elephant's skin, then emerged into the choppy sunlight of the marsh, where it flattened and narrowed and finally disappeared altogether among reeds and cattails that were higher now than Molly's head, so lush and thick she could barely see the gleam of blue water beyond, where the circle of the pond had shrunk into itself during the summer drought.

She checked for a moment, looking for the best way in through the reeds. As she did so, she heard voices. She was in time, then.

All the minutes she'd been running, Molly had kept her mind clenched tight, willing herself not to think about what she might find once she got to the pond. Now, taking in the pleasant, conversational sound of the voices, hearing Mr. Warren's familiar little bark of laughter, she felt confusion crowding in upon her sense of urgency and dread.

Maybe the note hadn't meant what she thought it had; maybe she'd read it wrong because of the way she'd been worrying about the Warrens—not just today, Molly understood suddenly, but for weeks, maybe even months, ever since the day she'd first met them. She hesitated among the reeds, raising an uncertain hand to brush away the tears she hadn't even known she was crying as she ran.

A sharp, loud explosion—a gunshot. Molly ran for the pond, crying *No! No!* inside her head. She sprang onto a rock and then froze, trying to make sense of what she was seeing through the reeds. There was a gun, sure enough, but it was leaning against the trunk of the big willow tree, several yards from where the Warrens sat comfortably in its shade, down in a little hollow with their backs to her, like people enjoying a picnic. In fact, Mr. Warren was in the act of pouring something from a large green bottle into a pair of thin-stemmed glasses set carefully on the grassy bank beside him; now he was handing one of the glasses to Mrs. Warren—

A champagne cork, Molly thought, sinking back into the reeds. That was all it had been, that scary noise—the sound of a cork popping out of the neck of the bottle, a sound she'd only ever heard on TV but one that had nothing to do with guns or . . . But she didn't want to think the word, even quickly.

"To home," Mrs. Warren was saying, lifting her glass. She turned her head and smiled at Mr. Warren, who nodded and said quietly, "Yes, to home."

Molly told herself that now was the moment for her to stand up and let them know she was there, to say she'd been looking for them to say good-bye. She didn't have to mention finding the note; she could just pretend that coming down to the pond where they were having their picnic, or whatever it was, had been an accident. Or she could say she'd remembered about its being Mrs. Warren's favorite place, even though she hadn't, not really, not until now. . . .

The Warrens were silent, sipping from their glasses and gazing across the pond, whose surface was wrinkled now by a small late-afternoon breeze that flickered through the narrow green-gold leaves of the willow branches overhead. Then Mr. Warren said, "I'm afraid I haven't been much of a manager, my dear. I suppose that's my main regret. Money, I mean. Went through an awful lot of it, had a good time doing it too, but never could seem to care much about the stuff. Did pretty well with other people's, I think, but when it came to our own—" He shook his head.

"Nonsense," Mrs. Warren said. "I wouldn't have had you any other way."

"Well, but all the same, it's what's brought us to this pass."

"Not entirely. There was Ruth. . . . Besides, we agreed

we weren't going to think of it that way—as a pass. Except in the literal sense, of course." Mrs. Warren lifted her shoulders in what Molly recognized as her old, humorous half-shrug. She was wearing the faded green denim skirt again, this time with a round-collared blouse printed with little blue and green flowers.

"Pour me another glass of champagne, would you, Duncan?" she said, and added dreamily, "I always did love being down here at this time of day. Remember when the children were small and we used to come down to the pond with our drinks before dinner? Martha would give them their supper, and then when we'd come back up, there they'd be in their pajamas, waiting for us on the lawn."

Mr. Warren nodded, while Molly made the picture in her own mind, too. He cleared his throat and said, "That's another thing. Drinking too much these last few months, I know. Kept telling myself it was because of the leg acting up again, but it wasn't that. It was other things hurting. Ruth going—not that there was ever much hope, of course—and then the house."

"Oh, my dear." Molly saw Mrs. Warren put her hand over his on the grass. "Of course. I know. But let's not think about all that. Let's think of what we've had, not what we've lost. And for pity's sake, let's not start apologizing to each other," she added with a laugh, "or we might be here forever." For a moment the words seem to hang in the bright air between them. "But for what it's worth, I'm sure I haven't been too easy to live with recently, either."

"When were you ever?" Molly could hear the smile in Mr. Warren's voice and then, as he shifted position to ease his leg, the frown with which he added, "But it rankles, you know, about the house. One thing to have to sell it, quite another to sell it to people who seem bent on ruining the place as fast as they can."

"Oh, Duncan, we've been through all that," Mrs. Warren said a bit sharply. "They simply don't know any better. After all, people with no background . . . But give them time. Sooner or later, they'll learn that new and glossy isn't necessarily better. They'll learn to let things fade and weather."

"Flashy little suburban fellow with his fancy sport shirts and computer wristwatch, or whatever the damn thing is," Mr. Warren said, as though he hadn't heard her. "Always yelling at me about something or other on the phone. Got the house dirt cheap, too."

"Yes, all right, but I still say it isn't as bad as you think," Mrs. Warren chided him. "Our Mr. Jackson has social ambitions as well as business ones, you know, and he's not stupid. I imagine he'll learn to do quite a good imitation of a country squire in the course of time—old tweeds and lots of leather and, who knows, maybe even a golden retriever at his heel, if the wife can be persuaded to do something about her allergies. Upward mobility, I believe it's called these days."

"Plain old social climbing, if you ask me," Mr. Warren said with a grunt. "Well, if you're right, they're going to be sorry they had the house all painted and papered up like a bandbox. All that's going to take a long time to weather."

"Yes. That flocked wallpaper up in our old bedroom, and white velvet curtains—to say nothing of the baronial dining room . . . Still, I give poor little Mrs. Jackson two years at most before she's out shopping madly for hooked rugs and English chintzes." Mrs. Warren shook her head. "I wonder what they have planned for the living room. Wall-to-wall carpeting, I'm sure, and everything matching, with lots of mirrors. But do you think they'll go in for those oversized lamps too, the kind that look like barrels wearing hats?"

They chuckled. Molly clenched her fists, a hot little lump burning in her throat. Of course she'd understood all along how the Warrens felt about her parents, but she hated hearing them say it out loud. Even worse, somehow, was knowing for sure that the Warrens really were the snobs her parents thought they were.

Mrs. Warren said thoughtfully, "The children, now, they're another story—much finer grained than the parents. Molly has natural good taste, I think, not that anyone's ever encouraged it; and from what you've told me, little Sean has a genuine feeling for the out-of-doors. The place isn't just a piece of expensive real estate to him, as it is to his father."

"Yes, nothing suburban about young Sean," Mr. Warren agreed. "Something of a free spirit, in fact. . . . Reminds me a bit of Peter at that age. Looks a bit like him, too." He cleared his throat. "More champagne, dear?"

"No, I think I've had all I want."

For a moment they were silent. The breeze had died, and the surface of the pond lay flat and burnished in the hot sunlight slanting through the trees.

"Well, then." Mr. Warren fumbled in the breast pocket of his shirt and tipped something small into the palm of his hand. "I wonder what the shelf life of these things is? Well, we'll soon find out."

He gave Mrs. Warren a tiny object—a pill, Molly thought it was, straining to see, while an alarm went off in her head like a siren. Mrs. Warren said, "If it doesn't work . . . promise me you'll do the other thing quickly," nodding her head at the gun leaning against the tree trunk, and Mr. Warren said, "Yes, my love, of course," and they clasped their free hands and—

"No!" Molly said, aloud this time, and hurtled from her rock, diving through the reeds to clamber up onto the bank of the pond.

The Warrens turned startled faces toward her.

"Why, Molly," Mrs. Warren said slowly, and let her hand fall, the one that still held the white pellet delicately pinched between her thumb and forefinger. "Whatever are you doing here? We didn't expect anyone. Are your parents—"

"I'm the only one here," Molly stammered, "but I saw the note. I know what you're going to do, but you can't! I won't let you!"

They exchanged a glance. "I don't think you quite understand, dear," Mrs. Warren began gently.

"But I do! There's something in those pills, isn't there? Something bad." Molly scrambled around on her knees to face them, brushing away the hanging willow fronds that clung to her wet cheeks, where the tears were rolling down again.

Mr. Warren sighed. "You'd better give me that for now, Virginia," he said, and dropped both of the little pills back into his pocket. He looked at Molly and said, "A form of cyanide, I believe, Molly. Had to carry them on us, back during the war—just in case, you know. One to a customer, but I took another off a friend of mine who . . . Well, never mind about that. Against regulations to have kept them, of course; in fact I can't quite think why I did—souvenirs of a sort, I suppose. At any rate, so quick as to be almost painless, or so we were given to believe."

"But why?" Molly demanded wildly. "Why would you want to die now, just when you're all ready to move into your cottage? With the brook and the rock garden and the beavers, I mean otters, and maybe not a whole lot of room, but enough so you can have your favorite things there, like the clock and the Japanese screen and the beautiful plates and—"

"There isn't any cottage, Molly," Mrs. Warren inter-rupted quietly. Molly stared at her, and she produced a tired little smile. "There never was. At least not any cottage that we could afford."

"But—"

"We did look," Mr. Warren assured her. "I expect we just about covered the county, didn't we, dear? But for what we could pay—" He shrugged. "Well, a gloomy couple of rooms in some jerry-built apartment building wouldn't have suited us at all, I'm afraid, nor a room over somebody's garage. Never could stand being cooped up, either of us. So we invented the cottage, you see—gave us a little more time to stay on while we thought what to do."

"But all the money my father's paying you for your house—" Molly shook her head in bewilderment. "You can't be that poor." When the Warrens merely exchanged amused glances, she said, "And anyway, there's Dick. Dick is rich —you said he was!"

"Oh, my dear, we wouldn't dream of taking anything from Dick," Mrs. Warren told her in a chilly voice. "As for being poor . . . haven't you ever heard of debts, Molly? By the time we finished paying off what we owed, we had virtually nothing left. Oh, a tiny yearly income and a bit of social security, but one can hardly live on that."

People did, Molly knew; but that didn't seem the important point right now. "But how could you owe that much money?" she said, sitting back on her heels. "Who did you owe it to?"

"Oh, mostly it was medical bills," Mr. Warren said, in his vague way. "Along with the usual butcher, baker, and candlestick maker, of course. . . . Here, Molly, have a wipe with this, why don't you?" He gave her the handkerchief that, as Molly knew, he always carried, and smiled kindly at her. "Now, now, don't carry on so. All for the best, that's what we feel. Sorry you had to happen in on things, though."

He spoke as if he expected Molly to run along now and leave them to take their suicide pills in peace, she thought dazedly. She said, looking from one to the other of them, "Medical bills . . . but you aren't sick."

"No," Mrs. Warren said. "But someone we cared about was, for a good many years, and needed special care. That's where most of the money went, Molly."

Molly shook her head. "Couldn't you have saved some out for yourselves, though? Or—what about your other children? What about Bud?" she said, remembering Mrs. Warren had said that Tory didn't have any money. "Bud would help you, wouldn't he? Or at least you could go live with him."

Mr. Warren turned his head away. Mrs. Warren gazed past Molly at the pond. At last she said, "Bud is dead, Molly. He and Paula and their son, Peter, died in an automobile accident nine years ago. Ruth survived, but there was severe brain damage. She never came out of her coma, which per-haps was merciful, but . . . but still, we hoped. And of course we were determined to see that she had the very best of everything—hospital care at first, then a private nursing home after the doctors said there was nothing more they could do for her."

Now her eyes met Molly's. They were glittering with unshed tears. "Nine years, Molly. She was twelve when it happened. She died this past April."

April. Molly's family had bought the Warrens' house in April.

"The house was always to go to Bud," Mrs. Warren went on. "We'd been renting it out, in the hope of accumulating some sort of nest egg for our old age. Unpleasant having strangers about the place, of course, but we thought of it as a temporary measure. Once Bud was ready to take it over, we planned to move down to North Carolina, where my sister was living at the time. She's gone now, of course."

Gone, Molly thought: gone meant dead. Mrs. Warren stirred, twisting a blade of grass between her thin fingers. "I suppose we ought to have sold the place back then, after the accident, but somehow we couldn't bear to. We had no idea at the time, of course, how long it would all go on, or how badly we'd have to let things go. . . . Dick helped at first with Ruth's expenses, but when the doctors said the support system ought to be turned off, he agreed with them. Do you understand what that means, dear?" Molly nodded. "He said we'd just be throwing good money after bad. Dear God, he actually said that."

Mr. Warren put a hand over his wife's, in the same gesture

she had used earlier. He said, "Now, Virginia, I don't think he meant it in quite the way it sounded. Also, he didn't know how tight things were becoming for us financially."

"And still doesn't," Mrs. Warren said, with something of her old sharpness. "Nor ever would, if I had my way. But I suppose it can't be avoided, once we're—once we've done what we mean to do."

Mr. Warren gave one of his sudden barks of laughter, startling Molly and sending a small bird twittering out of the upper branches of the willow tree. "Wish I could see Dick's face when that great van arrives," he said. "What do you suppose he'll do with a whole houseful of antique furniture in that glass egg carton of his? He'll be fit to be tied. Can't just sell it off, either—might show a lack of family feeling, his aged parents having departed this world so trag-ically, and so on."

Molly said wonderingly, "You sent all your furniture to Texas?"

He nodded, with an air of satisfaction. "Furniture, china, silver, the lot—every last carton. The things that were in the barn too; we had that put in storage while we were deciding what to do. . . . Well, had to send it somewhere, didn't we? All paid for, of course—the shipment, that is. All Dick will have to do is sign for it."

Both Warrens chuckled as if at a vast, rich joke.

"Couldn't you have sold the furniture if you needed money so bad?" Molly asked.

"Badly, Molly, not 'bad.' " Mrs. Warren corrected her automatically and gave a shrug. "Oh yes, we could have. It might have bought us a few years in a real cottage, or at least in a decent apartment somewhere, but that's about all.

Really, it hardly seemed worth it. And this way, at least the things will stay in the family."

"Cared for, if not loved," Mr. Warren agreed, with another dry chuckle. "Dick will see to all the repairs and restoration and so on—cost him a small fortune, but he'll do it. Too much of a perfectionist not to."

Seeing Molly's expression, Mrs. Warren said, "I'm afraid Molly thinks us rather frivolous, Duncan, either that or quite mad. Well, perhaps the two things go together—perhaps old age itself ought to be considered a form of madness."

Molly said, "But you're not old—not like that! I mean, you can still move around and do things, and you have friends and go to parties and . . . it's not like you can't take care of yourselves anymore. Not like the really old people that have to go live in those homes."

"Well, not for a while, at any rate," Mr. Warren agreed mildly. "But as for our friends, Molly—well, this may shock you, I'm afraid, but I suspect most of them will understand our decision perfectly well. It happens more often than most people suppose, suicide among the elderly. Usually a matter of sleeping pills." He shrugged. "We happen to have a quicker and surer method at hand, that's all."

Molly stared at them, aghast at how calm and ordinary they seemed in the face of the terrible, scary, final thing they intended to do. There wasn't anything unusual to notice about them except maybe for how thin they'd both gotten, Mr. Warren especially. Even his paunch seemed to have shrunk—he was wearing an old piece of rope threaded through the loops of his khaki pants, as if maybe his belts were all too big for him now.

A thought struck her, one that would have seemed horrible only a few minutes ago but that she now reached for almost eagerly. Mrs. Warren had said they weren't sick, but—

"You don't have cancer, do you?" she said. "I mean . . . well, is that why?"

Mrs. Warren smiled at her a little sadly. "No, Molly. At least not so far as we know. I realize we both look rather ghastly, but that's only because we've been working hard and not eating very much. Seemed ridiculous to go on spending money on food, as if we were geese to be fattened. . . . But it's true, that would have been a respectable reason, or at least one that other people would understand."

"Then why?" Molly said. "Why?"

"Because our real lives are over," Mrs. Warren told her calmly. "The pleasant, civilized lives we've been lucky enough to lead for the most part, allowing for some sadness and disappointment along the way. What's left is . . . scrabbling, pretending, making do. Ugliness. With, yes, probably a nursing home at the end of it all. Why should we have to accept that?"

She leaned forward and took both of Molly's hands in hers. How cold her skin felt, Molly thought, as if the heat of the summer day were something she had already sloughed off forever. "What you must try to understand, Molly," she said gently, "is that death doesn't hold the terror for us that it does for you. Oh, I admit I'm scared, but I really think I feel more curious than anything else. It will be an adventure, after all. And since otherwise our adventures seem to be over . . ."

She shrugged lightly, but her gray-green eyes were intent on Molly's, asking her to understand.

Not wanting to, refusing to, Molly snatched her hands away. She said desperately, "If it's about a nice place to live—well, they are going to build the senior citizen place, did you know that? My mom took around a petition, and the town had a vote, and it's going to happen. There'll be a lot of land left around the buildings, with trees and gardens and everything, and a special bus to take people shopping if they don't have cars, and it won't even cost very much. I guess it won't get done for a while, but my mom's committee is making a list of places senior citizens can stay if they need to, places that aren't usually allowed to be rented out—"

"More garage apartments," Mrs. Warren said with a nod. "I know."

"Thing is, Molly," Mr. Warren explained, almost apologetically, "we're spoiled, d'you see? Now, if we still had grandchildren, maybe it'd be worthwhile staying around, no matter how we had to live, or where. But since we don't, and since we can't stay on here . . . Even the cottage would have been a poor second best, I'm afraid. If it had ever existed, of course." He turned to his wife, his blue eyes brightening with amusement. "I must say, I was beginning to be rather taken with that cottage, Virginia."

"It was rather fun, wasn't it, making all that up? Putting in things we'd missed here. I'd even imagined a good spot for growing sweet peas—you know I never had any luck with them here—a trellis in a nice, cool corner by the kitchen door. . . . But otters, Duncan—really!" She laughed, shaking her head.

"Well, I thought if you could have your rock garden and so on, I could have my otters," Mr. Warren told her.

But Sean believed you, Molly thought. And so did I. She looked down at her grass-stained knees, thinking of Mrs. Warren's trowel still hanging in the garden shed, thinking she should have known right then what they were planning to do; and so she almost missed the quick exchange of glances between them, and the long shallow breath Mrs. Warren drew in before she said softly, "So now, Molly, will you leave us? Just go up to the house, and try not to think about . . . about what's happening here. Can you do that, do you think? It's a hard thing to ask of you, I know. But it's what we want."

When Molly didn't answer, simply staring at them while she prayed to wake up right now, right this next minute, because this couldn't be real, it could only be a bad nightmare she'd dreamed, Mr. Warren cleared his throat and said, "And while you're at it, Molly, perhaps you'd take the bottle and glasses up with you and dump them with the rest of the trash." He gave a little laugh. "Always seem to be asking you to take out the trash, don't I? We thought the cham-pagne added a rather stylish note, but . . ."

"Yes," Mrs. Warren agreed, making a face. "The effect is more dissolute than anything else, I fear."

Thoughts were chasing themselves frantically through Molly's head. How long had it been since Mom had dropped her off—a half hour? An hour? But even if she came back sooner than she'd planned, she wouldn't know where Molly was. Even if she went into the Warrens' side of the house, she still wouldn't know, because Molly had taken the note with her. She could feel it now, crumpled up in the pocket of her shorts.

Well, then, maybe she should at least tell the Warrens

that her mother might be here any minute now, that she'd be out looking for Molly . . . but no, that might just make them take the pills even sooner. The best thing to do would be to run back up to the house right now, as fast as she could go, and call the emergency number. They'd send an ambulance, and maybe they'd still be in time, in spite of what Mr. Warren had said. Then she remembered that the phone was disconnected.

The Warrens sat quietly watching her, waiting.

Molly said, "I had a present for you. One of the pool tiles that I fixed up, a dolphin one. I made a frame for it. I thought maybe you could hang it up somewhere in the cottage." She tried to remember where she'd left the present—on the front step, was that where? But anyway, of course, there wasn't any cottage. There wasn't any place at all where the Warrens would ever hang her tile. Molly hung her head, letting the tears splash down onto the pink cotton of her new top, which was all rumpled and dirty now anyway, its threads snagged by briars and the rough, sharp edges of the reeds.

"What a lovely thought, Molly." Mrs. Warren's voice was unsteady, and Molly looked up quickly, hopefully; but if her expression had changed for a moment, it was composed and calm again. "As a matter of fact, we had a present for you too—I almost forgot. I'm afraid it's not a very personal kind of present; in fact it's more for your parents than for you, except that I couldn't quite bring myself to hand it over to them outright. . . . At any rate, it's the chandelier for the dining room. You'll find it in a big carton there, with your name on it."

"Devil of a thing to pack," Mr. Warren observed. "Did it myself, when we put it away some years ago. Better take your time unwrapping it, Molly, or all those blasted little diamond-shaped bits of glass will get themselves in a tangle again."

"I always thought it a rather ornate piece myself, for a country dining room," Mrs. Warren remarked critically. "But no doubt your parents will be delighted with it."

Molly looked at them, sitting together under the canopy of the willow tree, Mrs. Warren with her hands clasped loosely around her drawn-up knees, Mr. Warren with his legs stretched out, leaning his weight on his good hip. He wore soft old hunting boots, worn and rubbed at the toes, but of good quality, like everything else the Warrens owned. She saw that they meant what they said. They wouldn't do it as long as she was there, but as soon as she left them, they would.

She shook her head. "I don't think we'll be using the chandelier," she said slowly. "I don't think we'll be living here, not after this. Not in your house."

Mr. Warren frowned. "Well, now, Molly, I guess I can understand how you might feel about that, but I don't expect your parents will feel quite the same way. A bit of a shock to them, of course, but they wrote us off a long time ago as a couple of arrogant old fools. And they've got a lot of money and effort invested in the place. Uncomfortable publicity for a time, perhaps, but after all, we're nothing to do with them—not their responsibility, just some crazy people from whom they happened to buy a house. It'll all die down soon enough."

"No," Molly said. She pushed herself to her feet. "All the happiness will be gone. For Sean and me, and maybe for my parents too. It will all be ruined. You said in the note that you wanted us to be happy growing up here."

She looked at Mrs. Warren, who nodded. That was what

she had written at the end of the note, after saying she hoped the children wouldn't judge them too harshly for what she and Mr. Warren were about to do. "I hope they will be happy growing up in this house," she'd written. "It embodies, of course, a way of life that has all but vanished. Still, it may yet have something to say to those who are willing to listen." And then she'd signed her name: "Yours sincerely, Virginia C. Warren."

"Well, now we can't be happy," Molly told her. "Not ever."

"Oh, Molly." Mrs. Warren shook her head, giving Molly an affectionate little smile. "You'll forget us in time—of course you will."

"But I want to remember you!" Molly cried. "I want to think of it all going on—you and Bud and Tory and Dick, even if you don't like him, and your grandchildren too, Ruth and Peter, when they'd come to visit and go swimming and throw the Frisbee. Now it'll be me and Sean instead, but all part of the same thing, the same place. . . ." She turned away blindly. "If you were going to kill yourselves, why did you have to do it here?" she said. "Why couldn't you go somewhere else? Why couldn't you go to a motel or something?"

 THIRTEEN

THERE WAS A silence. It stretched and spread and deep-
ened, but there was a pulse in it, too, like wings beating in
the air. Hearing it, Molly turned back. Through the blur of
her angry tears, she saw the Warrens gazing at her with
stunned expressions.

"A motel," Mrs. Warren repeated at last. "I can't say the
idea appeals to me very much."

"No," Mr. Warren agreed. "Sounds a trifle melodramatic,
doesn't it? Rather nasty, cheap melodrama at that—the orange carpeting, don't you know, and a factory watercolor
on the wall. . . . But she's right, you know. Molly is right."

"I suppose she is."

"The old place. . . ." Mr. Warren swung his head around,
blinking. "Why, we love this place, don't we? That's what
it's all been about, in a way. This idea of ours . . . it seemed
so right, somehow, so peaceful, here on our own land, planning how we'd see the pond last thing. . . . But selfish, I see
that now. We didn't really think what it would do to the
place itself. Or . . . trying to take it with us, maybe. Was
that part of it?"

He looked inquiringly at Mrs. Warren, who had bowed her head and wrapped her arms tightly across her chest. She nodded. "Yes. Perhaps so."

Molly said, "I know you don't like my parents very much. You think they don't have any—taste, or whatever, and they don't really care about the house. But they do. They wouldn't have bought it if it hadn't been . . . special, and different." Suddenly she was sure this was true, even if it was something her parents didn't yet realize themselves.

But the Warrens hardly seemed to be listening. Mr. Warren was pushing himself stiffly to his feet, holding out a hand to Mrs. Warren. "Come along, dear. A bad mistake, this would have been. Can't think why we didn't see it before. Now, if we'd been able to make it look like an accident . . ."

Mrs. Warren said in a low, fierce whisper, speaking only to herself, it seemed, "Oh, but this is what I wanted. I didn't want to have to go on. I don't want to." She raised her head and gave Molly a long, level look from beneath her dark brows, a look that made Molly want to flinch; but she didn't; she held herself steady, meeting the look. "Did you mean that about remembering, Molly?" Mrs. Warren asked slowly. "Was that why you wanted to look at our pictures—at the photograph album?"

Molly nodded.

"I see." Mrs. Warren sighed. "Well, of course, that makes a difference."

Then at last she took the hand Mr. Warren was extending and stood up, brushing bits of grass from the back of her her skirt. "Do stop eyeing the pond, Duncan," she said, and now her voice sounded more irritable than anything else. "I hardly think we can contrive a convincing accidental drowning in two feet of water."

Molly blurted out, remembering something, "That time when we thought Sean might be down here—that something might have happened—" She paused, not quite knowing how to ask the question.

But Mrs. Warren seemed to understand. "Because of Peter," she said with a nod. For a moment her gaze was blank and distant. "The car went off a bridge, did I mention that? It swerved to avoid a bus that was stalled halfway, and there was ice—not much, but enough. At any rate, he was thrown clear somehow when the car went into the river. His parents were killed outright, but Peter . . . Peter drowned."

She paused, squaring her shoulders under the thin fabric of her blouse. "We never talked about it, Duncan and I, but just at first I suppose there was a tendency to think of the two of you—you and Sean—as replacements for our grandchildren, in a way. Your coloring, the relationship in age and height and so on, and of course seeing you running about the place, hearing your voices . . ." For just an instant her eyelids quivered, but she lifted her chin and finished lightly, "But of course you're not replacements for anybody, are you? You're your own selves, and a good thing, too."

She stooped to pick up the champagne bottle and gave it a little shake. "Pity to waste good French champagne, but I suppose it's gone flat by now, in this temperature. . . . Would you bring the glasses, please, Molly?"

Molly nodded distractedly. She looked at Mr. Warren's shirt pocket, where the pills still were. "What will you do?" she asked. "You won't really go to a motel, will you? I didn't mean I *wanted* you to, only—"

"Of course, dear," Mrs. Warren said. "We understand. Well, no, I don't think so, at least not to kill ourselves. Far too sordid. And think how long it might be before anyone found us."

She emptied the bottle onto the grass. The clear liquid bubbled and hissed and then vanished without a trace. Gingerly, Molly picked up the two tulip-shaped glasses by their slender stems, then jumped at a noise from the pond. She turned her head in time to see a large turtle plop into the water from a big flat rock and swim slowly off into the reeds at the far end.

Mr. Warren frowned and said, "Was that a snapper, I wonder? Thought I'd got 'em all." His glance went to the gun resting against the tree trunk. "Better tell your father to take a good look around next spring before he stocks the pond, Molly. Snappers'll make a meal out of any fingerlings he puts in."

Molly watched him pick up the gun and thrust it casually under one arm. If Mom's here already, she thought, if she sees us coming up from the pond with the gun, I can just tell her Mr. Warren was taking a last shot at a snapping turtle. As for the champagne bottle and glasses—well, they'd just look like part of the farewell picnic Molly had thought for an instant it was.

Mrs. Warren was already making her way into the reeds, setting her sandaled feet down carefully as she felt out the path. Molly hurried after her, feeling more bewildered than scared now. Only a little while ago, everything had seemed to be happening in slow motion; now it seemed to be going too fast for her to catch up with.

"Where will you go?" she said anxiously to Mrs. Warren's back.

"Well, always supposing there's any gas in the car, I

imagine we can either find some scenic spot by the side of the road and finish what we set out to do, or . . ."

She slowed and came to a standstill, holding the empty champagne bottle by its neck and gazing off into the woods, where the sunlight hung like a veil among the leaves, dusting the air with gold. "Or we can go to Dick."

"Plenty of gas, dear," Mr. Warren assured her, limping up behind Molly. "Half a tank. In fact, I'd been fretting about leaving so much behind. Poor planning, you know." He gave a heavy sigh. "Well, yes, that always was a possibility. Still is, I suppose. He can hardly turn us away."

Mrs. Warren gave a harsh little laugh as she moved forward again, the path winding uphill into shade around the giant gray rock—a glacier rock, Molly remembered, left there by an Ice Age millions of years ago. "Oh, my dear, anything but," she said over her shoulder. "He'll install us in a suite of our own, I'm sure—or build one for us, if necessary— and see that we lack for nothing. Incidentally impressing all and sundry with his generosity and filial devotion. Good for his image, as I believe they say nowadays."

They were coming to the gap in the stone wall. Molly ran ahead to hold back the long whips of a blackberry vine, clutching the champagne glasses carefully in her free hand.

"Thank you, dear," Mrs. Warren said, and paused again, running the back of her hand across her forehead. "My, it's hot, isn't it? Do you know, Duncan, I'm feeling a bit shaky all of a sudden. What's the state of our remaining finances? Enough to run to a good dinner at the Inn, do you think? And a bed there too, for that matter? I really think we'd better have a good night's sleep if we're going to drive all the way to Texas."

"Well, let me see—there's the money I'd set aside for our funerals; won't be needing that now. Let Dick do the honors when the time comes, eh? And then I left a few hundred dollars in the checking account, more or less on principle. Everything else for Tory, of course, but that's in the papers in the van, and anyway doesn't arise as long as we're alive and kicking. As we seem to be."

"In a manner of speaking." Mrs. Warren gave another harsh-sounding laugh, and seemed about to say something more, then glanced at Molly and didn't; merely lifted her shoulders in a shrug and let them fall again.

"I'd say we're all right for immediate expenses," Mr. Warren went on, squinting into the treetops. "In fact, we might even linger a bit on the way, if you like. Unless, of course, we want to try and beat the van." He slapped at a mosquito. Somewhere deep in the woods a bird was singing, a long silvery song that rose and fell, asking a question, answering it, asking it again. "Listen—a thrush," he said, and Mrs. Warren nodded.

Molly studied their faces anxiously to see if they really meant what they said about going to Texas or if maybe it was just an act they were putting on for her benefit, to keep her from worrying anymore. Or it could be that they were just playing with the idea, she thought, the way they'd played with the idea of the cottage in Ludbury.

Mr. Warren cleared his throat. "On the other hand," he said, "that might rather spoil the effect, don't you think?"

"Yes," Mrs. Warren agreed slowly; and although they hadn't looked at each other, only stood motionless for a moment listening to the singing bird, Molly felt that something had been settled between them. "Yes," she said again, and this time her laugh had a ring of genuine amusement in it, as if something were funny after all. "I rather like the idea of the wordly goods arriving first, and then, after an interval, the aged parents. Preferably in the middle of a storm."

"On a dark and stormy night—yes, very good. . . . We might actually manage a hurricane, come to think of it— getting to be the season down there now, I believe. . . ."

They moved forward again through the break in the wall, picking their way carefully over the scattered stones, avoid- ing the poison ivy that tumbled down on either side. Molly stared at their bent heads as she followed along behind, wondering if she ought to feel sorry for Dick. Had the War- rens even thought how he'd feel when he found out his parents had killed themselves far away in Connecticut, with- out even giving him a chance to help them first? And now it sounded as if they were going to do their best to embarrass him and make life miserable for him. Being Dick, of course, she thought uncertainly, he might not even notice.

But then, as Mrs. Warren straightened up, Molly saw that in spite of her laughter and her joky words, there was no trace of humor in her expression. Her eyes were bleak beneath lids that looked suddenly old and hooded, like a reptile's, and her mouth was set in a flat, unsmiling line that Molly had never seen before.

She hurried to catch up, putting herself almost in Mrs. Warren's path, and looked up into her face. "Will it really be so bad?" she stammered. "Living with Dick, I mean?"

"Dear Molly," Mrs. Warren said, and her mouth relaxed a little. She reached down to smooth the limp damp hair from Molly's forehead. "You really are growing those bangs out, aren't you? Pretty soon you'll be able to keep them out of your face altogether. . . . No, it won't be so bad. Not if one doesn't mind saying thank you every single day of one's life. Unfortunately, we never did like being beholden, Duncan and I."

She glanced up at the house lying serene and gracious above the sweep of lawn, its windows reflecting the sky. "A pity about the flower beds," she said, as if to herself; and Molly understood that all along Mrs. Warren had expected her garden to die. Her gaze lingered on the house for a long moment. Then she drew it back to her husband, and her expression changed.

"Oh, Duncan, just look at you, with that ratty piece of clothesline around your waist and those terrible old pants! And look at me, for that matter, in this dreary skirt—though I did at least think to wear my nice old McMullen blouse for the occasion." She gave a little laugh, but her voice was shaky as she said, "Do you realize that all our clothes are on that van, every single stitch we own? They may simply refuse to take us in, down at the Inn."

" 'Course they won't," Mr. Warren said dismissively. "Old customers, after all, even if it has been a number of years since we've dined there. We'll just explain that we're in the middle of a move. Only the truth, after all." He shifted the gun to his other arm and took Mrs. Warren's elbow as they started forward over the rough ground at the bottom of the orchard. "We can buy a change of clothes tomorrow somewhere. Anyway, at our age, people don't much notice what one wears. . . . You know, Virginia, I've been thinking we might spend a night on the way at that rather grand old hotel in Tennessee, or was it Kentucky, where we stayed

with the Tremaines back in nineteen fifty-two—can't remember its name—"

"It was in Kentucky, I think, if the place still exists. But
anyway, that won't be on our route, Duncan. We'll be going
quite a bit south of there, surely."

"No, no, right on the way, I'm almost sure. I've got a map
in the car; I'll show you. Might even stop off and see the
Endicotts in Louisville too, come to think of it. They both
still alive?"

"Let me see. . . . Stephen died several years ago, I
believe—heart, I seem to remember, or maybe it was a
stroke—but Priscilla sent us a card last Christmas. A bit
dotty sounding, but then Priscilla always was rather . . .
fey, is that the word?—so one can't necessarily judge by
that. That she's still all there, I mean. Anyhow, plenty of
money still, I gather. I wonder if she's kept that cook she
used to have, the one who made those heavenly fritters,
remember, like little clouds?"

"Croquettes, weren't they? And I wouldn't have called
Priscilla fey, exactly. Charming woman, I always thought.
A bit scatty at times, to be sure, but more brains than most
people gave her credit for."

"Oh, Duncan, that was just her eyes! You always were
a pushover for big hazel eyes with lots of sticky black eyelashes. And of *course* they were fritters—corn fritters, served
with maple syrup. . . ."

Making plans, arguing about routes, discussing old friends,
the Warrens threaded their way slowly up the slope among
the apple trees. Molly followed at a little distance, feeling
the grass brush cool and silky against her bare ankles now
that she was no longer running, no longer scared. She looked

down at the pair of champagne glasses she still held by their brittle stems, wondering if the Warrens would want to take them with them. If they didn't, she thought, she would just as soon throw them away with the rest of the trash, as Mr. Warren had asked her to do earlier, even though they were beautiful glasses, delicate and fine and fragile, and probably quite a bit stronger than they looked.

As she raised her head again, she noticed for the first time how faded and washed out the boards of the old red barn looked against the fresh black paving of the driveway. The barn needed painting, she thought; either that, or the drive-way needed weathering.

"Molly, what are your flip-flops doing out on the roof?" her mother asked the next day, pausing in the upstairs hall-way with an armload of Molly's winter clothes that she was taking to hang in the closet in Mrs. Warren's room. "Don't you know you're not supposed to play out there until we get that rail built up higher? It's dangerous."

"No it's not," Molly told her. "Not if you're careful. Anyway, I don't think we should change the railing. It would look funny if it was any higher."

"Molly—" She frowned, noticing at the same time how Molly had grown and thinned down over the past few months. The planes of her face were beginning to define themselves, her cornflower-blue eyes to lose the vague, soft, cloudy look of childhood. Her gaze was clearer and more intent, with a cool little light in it sometimes that was just a bit disconcerting.

"Not from up here, from outside," Molly explained. "If you stand down on the lawn, you can see what I mean. The railing is exactly right the way it is."